The woman was trouble.

He glanced at her in the passenger seat. But she also intrigued him. Not that he'd do anything about it. Chloe had too many secrets, including her identity.

Ethan hit a deep rut in the mountain road and she groaned. "I guess a city girl like you isn't used to roughing it," he said.

She snorted. "You'd be surprised at some of the places I've been to."

He jumped on that clue. "Tell me."

The blood drained from her face.

The cabin came into view and he tabled his interrogation. Right now he needed to get some answers from its owner. "Stay in the car while I go in." He opened the car door and a bullet whizzed over the top of his head. "Get down!"

"This is starting to tick me off."

Ethan couldn't believe it. Someone was shooting at them and she wasn't afraid? "What kind of life have you really led?"

Chloe didn't answer.

Didn't matter. Either way, that life was now his to protect.

Liz Shoaf resides in North Carolina on a beautiful fifty-acre farm. She loves writing and adores dog training, and her husband is very tolerant about the amount of time she invests in both her avid interests. Liz also enjoys spending time with family, jogging and singing in the choir at church whenever possible. To find out more about Liz, you can visit and contact her through her website, www.lizshoaf.com, or email her at phelpsliz1@gmail.com.

Books by Liz Shoaf

Love Inspired Suspense

Betrayed Birthright
Identity: Classified

IDENTITY: CLASSIFIED

LIZ SHOAF

HARLEQUIN® LOVE INSPIRED® SUSPENSE

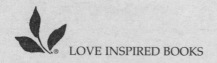 LOVE INSPIRED BOOKS

Recycling programs for this product may not exist in your area.

ISBN-13: 978-1-335-67889-8

Identity: Classified

www.Harlequin.com

Printed in U.S.A.

And he said unto them, Go ye into all the world, and preach the gospel to every creature.
—*Mark* 16:15

To my own hero, Captain James W. Phelps. Over the years we have traveled the long and winding path that God set us upon. There's been laughter and tears, but no matter what, we always knew God was there every step of the way, ready to catch us if we fell. I have no doubt that you love me, and that's a very precious commodity.

To my editor, Dina Davis, who never fails to catch my plot problems. :) Thanks for being in my corner! And to her boss, Tina, who has final approval of all books. The art department always does such a fantastic job, so a shout-out to all you guys who work behind the scenes to make every book possible.

ONE

Chloe Spencer tossed a piece of popcorn high into the air and deftly caught it in her mouth. A barely audible whimper rose from the vicinity of the floor beside her office chair. She glanced down and grinned. "Want some, do you, Geordie?"

Her fifteen-pound chocolate miniature poodle stared at her with black button eyes, bright with intelligence. He gently took the snack she handed to him.

Her computer chirped. She swiveled her chair around and rubbed her hands together in anticipation. As head of her one-person security company, Spencer Security, her job was to find and eliminate cyber threats and in-house data theft for companies she had contracted with. Sci-Fi Works Corporation was one of her clients, and a board member suspected someone in the company of stealing data and selling it to outside sources. He personally asked her to look into it on the sly.

She hit a few keys to activate her webcam, and there sat CEO Peter Norris, right in front of his computer in his office. She had a perfect shot of him. Geordie snorted and she grunted back.

Chloe quickly triggered the hidden software installed on all computers within the company—approved by the same board member—which allowed her to view and record anything an employee did on their PC. She also turned on her own camera and recorded everything she did—a security measure that protected her against a disgruntled employee accusing her of planting evidence.

"Yeah, yeah, I know he's way out of my league, but he's not my type anyway."

Out of her league? That was putting it mildly. She didn't live in the same universe as Peter Norris, the head of Sci-Fi Works Corporation. He was wealthy, successful and, from the information she'd gleaned in a routine computer search, a nice and straight-up kind of guy. And her? Well, she lugged around a ton of baggage. Her background wasn't exactly what anyone would call squeaky clean, which was why she was sitting home on a Friday night instead of out on a date. She'd probably never marry because she would never tell anyone the reason she had spent time in juvenile hall. Her past held secrets and she meant to keep them.

Propping her elbows on her desk, Chloe found herself held spellbound by Peter Norris's stunning dark blue eyes—even though she wasn't personally interested—when a knock on his office door reverberated through her computer's sound system. She sat up straight and stared at the screen, curious to see who had arrived. A colleague? A late date with a beautiful woman? A partner in crime, helping him sell company secrets?

The sound of a door opening and closing reached her, and not long after that, a heated argument ensued between two men. She turned up the volume on her PC and Geordie whimpered. She reached down and gave him a soothing pat, keeping her eyes glued to the computer screen.

"Come on, get in front of the webcam so I can see what's going on," she murmured to herself.

Two men were shouting at each other, but she couldn't quite make out what they were saying. Her throat constricted when she heard a loud thump. Were they having a fistfight? Mr. Norris's body flew past the screen and disappeared, and she heard him hit the floor with a solid thud. Chloe jumped out of her chair and leaned closer to the screen. She jerked back when a hand rose into view and pointed a wicked-looking gun toward the floor near the desk, the direction Mr. Norris had fallen.

"No! This can't be happening," she whispered.

The sound of a soft pop filled the room. She reached for the chair behind her as a few tiny red splatters hit Peter Norris's computer camera, enlarging themselves on her screen. Easing into a sitting position, Chloe's blood ran cold when a ski-masked face stared at her through the small droplets of blood.

"Yes, he's dead, Miss Spencer. You've been a hard woman to track down. The long delay has cost me a lot of time and money. I'm not happy about that." He moved his face closer to the webcam. His gritty voice scraped her nerves with its intensity. "I decided to give you a taste of what's in store for you if you don't give me the disc. I would advise you to get it now. My deliveryman should be at your door any second." He turned away but glanced over his shoulder with menace in his eyes. "I wouldn't advise contacting the police, or Stan will find himself in the same position as Peter Norris."

The screen went blank, and through her haze of terror, Chloe vaguely registered that the killer had logged off Peter Norris's computer.

A loud, piercing bark jolted her out of shock. She tore her gaze away from the now-blank screen and looked down at her dog. "Geordie," she whispered, "we're in big trouble and I don't even know what he's talking about. I'll worry about the disc later. Right now, we have to get out of here."

Her heart was pounding and her mind racing. The killer's so-called deliveryman could be at her door any second, and she needed time to figure out what he wanted and how he knew so much about her.

"Geordie, grab your stuff." Her poodle was highly trained and must have sensed her urgency. He skidded out of her office and headed toward the kitchen, where she kept his stuff in a bag.

Chloe left her laptop and smartphone where they were—she could be tracked through the technology—and grabbed several burner phones she stored in her desk. Being a computer geek came in handy. Chloe met Geordie in the foyer and tore open the closet door. Having learned a lot during her *forced* tenure at the FBI, Chloe had a "go" bag ready for any emergency that might arise. It included a new identity, passport, driver's license, the works.

She threw on her leather jacket, slipped the strap of the duffel over her shoulder and opened the door to her apartment. She locked it quickly after her dog followed her out. Peering at the elevator in the middle of the hallway, she saw the numbers were moving upward toward her floor. "It's the stairwell for us, Geordie," she whispered. They were halfway to the exit door when the elevator dinged. She glanced over her shoulder as a masked man stepped off the elevator, saw her fleeing and started running toward them.

His hand reached inside his leather jacket and Chloe slowed down. She'd never make it to the garage and her Harley. She lowered her right arm, and the knife she kept stashed up her sleeve dropped into the palm of her hand. Before the guy had a chance to lift the gun, Chloe turned midstride, lifted her arm and threw the knife. It landed exactly where she wanted it to, in his right arm. He stumbled, dropped the gun, grabbed his bleeding arm and shot her a look filled with rage.

Chloe didn't wait to see if he followed. She pushed the stairwell door open, and she and Geordie raced down to the garage. She lifted her dog, placed him in the attached pouch strapped to the back of the seat and straddled the bike. The roar of the engine filled the parking deck. She quickly maneuvered the bike around and shot forward. Just as she was passing the stairwell door, it opened, and the killer took aim. Chloe swerved the Harley sharp into a curve and almost laid the motorcycle on its side. Two bullets bit into the concrete above her. As soon as the bike was upright, she headed for the exit.

They hit the street and Chloe rode around for a short time, making sure they weren't followed. She'd stop at an internet café and send an anonymous email reporting the crime. She couldn't do it under her own name because there was a chance the FBI would become involved due to the high-profile murder. She couldn't take a chance on the killer going after Stan.

She didn't even consider contacting Stan. As Director of Criminal Cyber, Response and Services Branch of the FBI, he would end up in the middle of this mess, and she refused to take that chance. Stan and Betty had assumed custody of, and later adopted, a sassy sixteen-year-old girl who had hacked into a bank and gotten sent to juvenile hall. Thanks to Stan, and her extensive hacking skills, the judge wisely, and leniently, allowed her to leave juvenile hall and finish out her sentence working for the FBI cyber unit. Her community service helped the FBI and taught her a lesson at the same time. And, of course, all child labor laws were strictly adhered to.

Stan and Betty had done enough for Chloe already. She had to handle this herself. She'd call them after she decided where she was heading and tell them she and Geordie had taken a little vacation. Risking their lives by involving them wasn't an option.

Standing on the sidewalk outside of Lucy's Café, enjoying the unusually warm late-autumn weather, Sheriff Ethan Hoyt almost spit out the mouthful of coffee he'd just taken when a Harley roared down the street, then swerved into a spot right in front of him. The rider removed her helmet after pushing down the kickstand, then she attached the helmet to the motorcycle and ran her hands through short, midnight-black hair, leaving it spiked all over her head.

His eyes narrowed as he scanned her face and took note of every feature. Pixie face with porcelain skin, narrow nose, sculpted chin, brown eyes, black eyebrows. She had the physique of a runner, he noticed as she lifted a leg over the seat of the bike and shot him a mischievous grin. Two dimples appeared on either side of her mouth, contrasting with the biker-dude appearance. She was a looker, but he wasn't the least bit interested. He had a daughter to raise, and he had failed to make his deceased wife happy when she was alive.

When she unzipped a partially open attachment on the back of the bike, he took what he hoped appeared to be a casual sip of coffee. She placed both hands inside the leather pouch and lifted something out.

He was totally caught off guard when she folded a small, ugly brown dog into her arms. Ethan didn't like surprises. He liked to think of himself as being prepared for every contingency. She crooned nonsense to the mutt and placed him on the ground, where he promptly pooped on town property. She praised the critter for doing what nature demanded, then dug around in another bag and lifted a leash triumphantly in the air. After attaching it to the dog's collar, she approached the sidewalk.

Ethan's eyebrows shot up when he spotted the studded leather dog collar. The thing appeared to be a poodle and it looked as harmless as a flea. His eyes narrowed behind his sunglasses when she flashed him a big smile before sauntering past, decked out in black leather pants, jacket and biker boots. His gut—that had never failed him—screamed the woman and her sidekick were trouble. He hadn't missed the wariness in her eyes she tried to hide behind the big friendly smile.

Taking several long strides to catch up with her, Ethan slapped a hand on the door leading to Lucy's Café, effectively stopping her when she tried to pull it open. "Ma'am, you can't leave dog poop on the ground. We have city ordinances."

She lifted her head slowly, an anticipatory gleam in her eyes. "I wouldn't move if I were you."

Ethan went on high alert and glanced at her hands for weapons, but they were empty. It was then he noticed she had dropped the leash. A low growl, very close to his right ankle, rose from below him. He removed his arm from the door and the growl turned into a snarl. Without moving, he glanced down. The previously friendly looking little mutt had his gums peeled back, revealing a mouthful of sharp, pointed teeth.

The woman had the audacity to chuckle before snapping out a command.

"Geordie! Off!"

In a split second, the small—Ethan would put the dog at twelve to fifteen pounds—vicious beast closed his mouth and plopped onto his hind quarters, transforming back into the deceiving appearance of a sweet, docile dog. The thing was covered in brown curls. Ethan could barely see its beady little eyes, which were now warm and pleasant looking, as if the thing had never threatened to chew his leg off.

"I came here to grab a bite to eat. Now, are you going to call the police, or am I allowed to go inside the restaurant and get some paper napkins to clean up Geordie's mess? I ran out of poop bags several days ago."

Ethan took a deep breath. He'd just made a fool of himself and could only chalk it up to the sudden appearance of Dorothy carting Toto around on a motorcycle.

Time to back up and get some information. He wanted to know where she was from. Evidently the woman and her companion had been on the road for several days. He flashed her an apologetic grin and held out his hand. "The name's Hoyt, Sheriff Ethan Hoyt," he said with relish. He tended to dress in jeans and a civilian shirt when he was on duty.

Her eyes widened for a mere moment after he introduced himself as sheriff. She quickly masked her reaction and shook his hand. "Name's Samantha Bailey."

Was that a slight hesitation in her voice when she said her name, or was it his imagination?

"Welcome to Jackson Hole, Ms. Bailey. You here on vacation? Visiting friends?"

She grabbed the leash off the ground and petted her dog before straightening and looking him in the eye. No wilting flower here.

"Are you the official welcoming committee for Jackson Hole? If so, you need to brush up on your etiquette."

Time to back off. Other than his gut tightening, he had no grounds to suspect her of anything, and he *was* being rude. "I do apologize."

He glanced down at the mutt. "I'm happy to hold on to your, uh, dog while you get some napkins to clean up his mess."

Her lips tightened. "His name is Geordie, and he's a highly trained, purebred male miniature poodle."

Ethan tried to appear suitably impressed, but the scraggly thing didn't look as if it had an ounce of testosterone backing up her claim that he was male. He barely heard what sounded like a small growl, and it hadn't come from the dog. He took the leash from Ms. Bailey, and she flung the door open and disappeared inside Lucy's Café.

He stared at the dog. "So where do you hail from, Geordie?" The dog's tail thumped on the sidewalk. "I caught a whiff of a Northern accent with a touch of Southern flavor from your mom. You from New York?"

"Are you interrogating my dog, Sheriff?"

His body jerked, and he felt like an idiot. It was an unfamiliar emotion. He never even heard her approach. The woman was light on her feet. He flashed her a big smile when he turned. "Just being cordial, ma'am."

She cleaned up the poop, took the leash from his hand, scooped up her dog and placed him back inside the black leather satchel.

"There's a nice bed-and-breakfast down the

street, if you plan on staying." Ms. Bailey intrigued him, and for some strange reason, he wasn't ready for her to move on if she was just passing through.

Throwing a leg over the Harley, she showed all her teeth. Not exactly a smile. "I did my research, Sheriff, and it so happens I have a reservation at Mrs. Denton's Bed-and-Breakfast. I'll grab something to eat later." Flicking the kickstand up with her left heel, she tugged the helmct onto her head. "And just so you won't worry, I'm here on vacation, but if I like it, I might stay a few weeks."

Frowning as she revved the motorcycle's engine, Ethan stood on the sidewalk and watched her travel two blocks and stop in front of Mrs. Denton's place. He took note of the motorcycle's New York tag.

Jackson Hole was a tourist town, and he was used to seeing all types of people come and go, but Ms. Bailey was an entity of her own. Was she an eccentric, wealthy elite with too much time and money on her hands? Or was she running from something? The only lead he had was the moment of wariness he saw in her eyes. That wasn't enough to suspect the woman of being up to no good, but his time spent as a high-ranking detective in Chicago had left its mark. He'd learned years ago to listen to his gut, and his gut was balled in a tight knot.

He paused on the sidewalk as a beige sedan slowed in front of Mrs. Denton's place and then picked up speed as it shot forward. It passed by him. Two large men sat in the front seats. They didn't even glance at him as they passed, but he noticed the New York plate. He pulled his pad and pencil out of his shirt pocket and wrote down both the car and motorcycle's tag numbers. Odds were the men were in Jackson Hole to hunt and fish, but it never hurt to check.

Interesting thing when two New York vehicles showed up in Jackson Hole within thirty minutes of each other. It was a long way for anyone to drive.

TWO

Chloe quickly opened the front door to the bed-and-breakfast and slipped inside with Geordie at her heels. Spinning around, she stole a glance through one of the glass panes bordering the door. The thick, old glass was wavy, but clear enough for her to catch sight of a large beige sedan whizzing down the street. She squinted and caught the New York tag but couldn't make out the number.

Her dog nudged his nose against her leg. She scanned the rest of the neighborhood through the window. "The car's from New York, Geordie. I felt eyes on us from the time we left Lucy's Café. You think the killer's hired toadies followed us from the city? I picked Jackson Hole because I don't know anyone here and it's clear across the country. I covered our tracks. Stan always claimed I was slippery as an eel."

While studying the surrounding area through the wavy glass, her thoughts were invaded by the sheriff's expressive face. She didn't want to admit—to herself, or her dog—that the good sheriff had shaken her up a bit. He was good-looking, no doubt about it. Well over six feet, dark hair cut short—not quite a military buzz cut, but close. He had sharp, intelligent green eyes. Chloe felt as if he saw deep inside her, past her facade, and was trying to dig up the grave of secrets she kept carefully hidden.

"And why would you need to cover your tracks, young lady?" a sharp voice said from behind her.

Reacting on pure adrenaline, in one smooth move, Chloe pulled the long, thin knife from her shirtsleeve and whipped around. The knife disappeared just as fast when she faced a little old lady who looked like a strong wind could knock her over.

Covering herself with oozing Southern charm, Chloe moved toward whom she assumed to be Mrs. Denton, proprietor of the bed-and-breakfast. "I'm Samantha Bailey. I apologize if I startled you. I have a reservation."

The stooped gray-haired woman, decked out in jeans and a plaid shirt, gave her a calculating look and grinned. Chloe didn't trust that grin. Not for one New York minute. No pun intended.

"I don't think so."

That didn't make sense. Maybe the woman was senile.

Chloe softened her tone. "I'm sorry. I'm not quite following you."

Her survival antennae went haywire. Chloe slid her hand behind her back and had grasped the doorknob, ready to flee, when Mrs. Denton gleefully dropped her bombshell.

"From what I overheard you say, I doubt that's your real name. Sounds like you'll be a handful, but I'm up for the job." The old lady's chest puffed out. "I fought off two ruffians several months ago. They were after one of my guests."

Chloe grinned when the older woman whipped a pencil-thin Taser out of her jeans pocket.

"Got one of the kids in town to order me this off the internet after that episode."

She admired the older woman's spunk, but Chloe couldn't stay here. Not if Mrs. Denton was suspicious of her name.

This situation had created a big problem. She'd already introduced herself to the sheriff as Samantha Bailey, and there would be more questions than she wanted to answer if he found out she had lied.

Just as her hand twisted the doorknob behind her, the door was jerked open from outside. Chloe spun around to face the threat, knife back in hand. With one eye on her knife and the other on Geordie, Sheriff Hoyt stopped on the threshold of the door. In the blink of an eye, Chloe slipped the knife back up her shirtsleeve, but Hoyt's sharp eyes hadn't missed a thing.

Mrs. Denton nudged Chloe aside and approached the law and order of Jackson Hole.

"Sheriff Hoyt, so good of you to call." She took him by the elbow and guided him inside.

Chloe girded herself. Her past was about the catch up with her. If Sheriff Hoyt discovered she had lied about her name, with his resources he'd discover her real name and try to find out about her past, which would raise more questions than she was willing to answer.

It took a moment before Mrs. Denton's words halted Chloe's urge to flee. She had no doubt that she could get away from the sheriff. Chloe took pride in her high success rate of escaping problematic situations.

"I was just welcoming Miss Bailey. Why don't we move to the kitchen and have a nice cup of coffee?"

Chloe released her breath. Mrs. Denton hadn't shared her suspicions.

The sheriff sighed and moved forward. It would have been rude not to with Mrs. Denton's death grip on his arm. Chloe was wondering just how feeble Mrs. Denton really was when the older woman looked over her shoulder and sent her a saucy wink.

Did she dare trust this elderly woman to keep her suspicions to herself?

After the tragic death of her parents when she was young, Chloe had only trusted four people in her life: Stan and Betty, of course. Then there was Sarah Rutledge. She ran the orphanage. Neither of her parents had had any living relatives, so they'd made a contingency plan for Chloe to go to the orphanage should anything happen to them. They had wanted to avoid the foster care system. And then there was Uncle Henry. He wasn't a blood relative, but he'd worked for Stan at the FBI for years before retiring and insisted Chloe call him "uncle."

If the sheriff Googled or ran a search on her real name, any computer hacker would be able to track her down and her life wouldn't be worth dirt because the killer would know where she was. The way she figured it, if he couldn't find her or get in touch with her, she'd have time to find the disc he wanted and hopefully keep everyone she loved safe.

Sheriff Hoyt and Mrs. Denton disappeared around the corner. If she wanted to vanish, this was her chance. The place between her shoulder blades itched—a warning system that never failed her—and she glanced through the wavy glass just as the sedan she'd spotted earlier rolled slowly back down the street.

She whipped around and leaned against the heavy wooden door. How had they found her? She was very, very good at covering her tracks. And then it hit her. The killer's minions had likely planted a tracking device somewhere on her bike.

She calculated her options and narrowed them to one. She'd have to make nice with the sheriff and trust Mrs. Denton long enough to check her mode of transportation for tracking devices. Moving toward the kitchen, she made her plans. She'd wait until everyone was asleep, check her Harley and leave. She'd hit the bank before getting out of New York, so cash wasn't a problem for the time being.

"Come on, Geordie, do your sweet dog thing and let's go charm the sheriff."

When Samantha Bailey didn't immediately follow them into the kitchen, Ethan had to force himself not to peel Mrs. Denton's fingers off his sleeve. For being so elderly, the woman had a strong grip. He relaxed when Samantha and her dog sauntered into the warm, inviting kitchen, but his suspicions were resurrected when the menacing little dog padded up to him and licked his hand, all sweet and charming.

"I keep coffee made for any guests who might wander in, so ya'll take a seat and we'll have us a nice chat."

Ethan sat at the oak table that had been there as long as he could remember, leaned his chair back on two legs and grinned. He wondered how Miss Biker Babe—he now knew she was a "Miss" thanks to Mrs. Denton—from New York would handle Mrs. Denton's sweet, Midwestern etiquette.

Sam—the shortened name seemed more fitting for such a feisty woman—grinned and pulled out a chair. "Why, thank you, Mrs. Denton, that's very gracious of you. Can I help you do anything?"

Surprise had him leaning forward and the front two legs of his chair slammed to the floor. A drawn-out, Southern accent flowed naturally off her tongue. The woman was an enigma. Mrs. Denton snorted a laugh when she turned and caught his surprise. "I've got it, but thanks for the offer."

The dog heaved a satisfied sigh and lay—docile as a lamb—at Sam's feet.

Three coffee mugs, along with a plate of cookies, were placed on the table. Mrs. Denton released an elderly-like sigh of relief when she sat down.

Ethan grabbed a warm chocolate chip cookie

and closed his eyes at the first taste of bliss. He'd been enjoying her baking ever since he was a young boy.

"Wow!"

His eyes popped open and he caught Sam stuffing the second half of a cookie into her mouth. She nodded at Mrs. Denton. "You ever think of selling these?"

The older lady grinned. "Matter of fact, I have, but I don't know how to go about it. I don't know a thing about those newfangled computers, and everyone says you have to get one of those websites to sell anything these days."

Sam leaned forward, an excited light in her eyes. "It's easy. All you have to do is set up a snazzy website and make sure you tag onto any other sites that will promote your cookies."

She sent a nervous glance toward Ethan, sat back and lifted her mug to her lips. After taking a sip, she carefully placed it on the table. "There are people you can hire to set that up for you."

Mrs. Denton turned to Sam and deftly changed the subject. "So you're here to see the sights?"

Was that a slight relaxation in Sam's posture, or was it Ethan's imagination?

"That's right. Geordie and I decided to take a vacation."

Mrs. Denton got a look in her eye that Ethan

had seen before, but she opened her mouth before he could stop her.

"Well, Sheriff Hoyt could show you around Jackson Hole. He grew up here before he moved to Chicago and became a hotshot detective. He's a widower, you know, married a sweet girl and came back here to raise his family, but Sherri died of cancer, leaving the poor man with a young daughter to raise."

Ethan froze in his chair as memories of his deceased wife rose to the surface and threatened to choke him. Some were good, a few weren't, and he took full responsibility for Sherri's unhappiness at the end of her life.

He didn't want to look at Sam—see the pity in her eyes—but he lifted his chin. What he saw surprised him. A unique understanding, as if she'd experienced something similar, but not an ounce of pity.

"Life's tough that way sometimes." That was all she said, and it felt just right.

He cleared his throat. "Yes, it is. How about you, Sam, you ever been married?" Time to start his fishing expedition because his gut was screaming that this woman had secrets.

Mrs. Denton piped up, "Sheriff, don't be rude to my guest."

His gaze slid back to Sam and he waited.

One black eyebrow arched. "Not that it's any

of your business, Sheriff, but it's just Geordie and me."

So the woman had perfected the art of evading a question. He decided to hit hard. "And what reason would a lady like yourself have for carrying a knife up the sleeve of her shirt?"

Mrs. Denton gasped, but Sam held up a hand. "It's okay, I'm happy to answer his question."

Mrs. Denton looked as interested in the answer as he did, even though she made the proper noises about him interrogating her guest.

"Let's just say I've been in several places that weren't very safe. Don't you think it's a good idea for a woman to be able to take care of herself?"

Ethan couldn't help but compare Sam to his late wife. Sherri had been born and raised in Chicago—a place full of crime—but somehow she had managed to hang on to her innocence. His wife had been soft and trusting. In comparison, Sam was wary and prickly as a porcupine. The woman had street smarts, which made him only more curious.

The front door slammed open and closed. In one fluid movement, Sam jumped to her feet, pulled a small gun from inside her leather jacket and pressed her back to the wall next to the open threshold leading to the kitchen. He was simultaneously shocked and impressed at her fast reaction, but when his daughter came running past Sam, his surprise turned to fear.

Penny saw him first and flew into his lap, wrapping her precious arms around his neck, preventing him from reaching for his weapon. He kept his eyes glued to the new woman in town, and, in a flash, Sam tucked away her weapon and seated herself back at the table. He started breathing again.

"Daddy, you'll never believe what happened at school today. Tommy Milton put a gross frog in my desk and I told him you'd put him in jail. He said a person couldn't go to jail for that, but that's not true, is it? 'Cause he deserves to be punished."

Ethan stared at his six-year-old blond-haired blue-eyed precious daughter and wondered yet again why he'd been so blessed to have this child. She was the spitting image of her mother and the reason he got out of bed each morning.

He didn't have a chance to respond because Penny squealed and wiggled out of his lap when she spotted the sweet-vicious dog. She got away from him and was on the floor with the animal before he had a chance to stop her. He held his breath, waiting to see if the beast would take a chunk out of his daughter, until a chuckle came from across the table.

He frowned at Sam.

"Don't worry. He won't hurt her. Geordie loves kids."

A knife, a gun, an attack poodle and a Harley. Ethan wasn't happy with the new visitor in town, but he couldn't question her in front of his daughter.

"Penny, how did you know I was here?"

Big, innocent blue eyes swung his way. "Daddy, I asked the bus driver to let me off at the station. Mrs. Armstrong told me you were here."

Mrs. Denton interrupted before he could reprimand his daughter for ditching her after-school babysitter.

"Have a cookie, Penny. They're fresh out of the oven."

His daughter scurried around the table, grabbed a cookie and stared at Sam.

"Who are you and is that your dog?"

Ethan took a small amount of satisfaction in Sam's discomfort as she stared at his daughter as if she'd never seen a child before.

"Um, my name is Samantha Bailey, and Geordie belongs to me."

"What kind of a dog is he? Can I come play with him tomorrow after school?"

Time to put a lid on his daughter's natural curiosity and find out more about Sam before Penny spent any future time with her.

"Penny, thank Mrs. Denton for the cookie. We should get you back to the sitter. She'll be worried sick when you don't get off the school bus at her house."

Penny focused adorable, pleading eyes on him. "You're not mad, are you, Daddy? I just couldn't wait to see you after school."

As always, his heart melted. "No, sweetie, I'm not mad. We'll talk about this when we get home."

Sam mumbled something under her breath. He gave her a sharp look. Did she just say what he thought she said?

"What was that?"

Her lips curved up at the corners, and her words came out sweet and syrupy. "I said one of my dogs would never get away with what your daughter just did."

That raised his hackles. Nobody criticized his daughter but him. "And what did my daughter just do?"

Sam gave Penny an apologetic glance. "Sorry, kid, but I know all the tricks." She looked back at Ethan. "Let's just say I train dogs on the side, and I know all about handling. We'll leave it at that."

Ethan was about to explode until he saw Penny's eyes narrow on Sam. Time to go. He'd seen that look before and it usually preceded an unsettling argument.

Maybe he had been too lenient, but Penny had lost her mother so young, and his daughter's tears just tore him up.

He rose and took Penny by the hand. "Thanks for the cookies, Mrs. Denton." He also acknowledged Sam. "I hope you enjoy your vacation."

He pulled Penny away from the dog and breathed a sigh of relief when they were outside. His daughter walked quietly beside him on their way back to the station. He tightened his hand on hers when he thought about Sam and the beige sedan and wondered if trouble had followed Miss Biker Babe to Jackson Hole.

THREE

It was after midnight, and Geordie's eyes followed Chloe as she dumped everything she had brought with her onto the bed. She checked every piece of clothing, searched every item of her toiletries and went through Geordie's supplies, but found no tracking devices. Not that she expected to. She would have known if someone had broken into her apartment. She had very good security, but she checked all her stuff anyway, just to be on the safe side. Throwing on her jacket, her dog followed her as she went outside and scoured her bike from front to back.

No tracking devices anywhere.

She reached down and scratched Geordie behind the ears. He grunted and she grinned.

"Whatcha think? Should we move on to safer pastures, or stay here and find out who those two men in the beige sedan are? It could be they're harmless. Just two men on vacation."

Her dog grunted.

"Yeah, I don't think so, either. As Stan always says, there are few coincidences in life. Well, there's only one way to find out. Let's get you back inside and I'll pay our New York friends a little middle-of-the-night visit and see what's what. Maybe they know something about the disc."

Geordie knew the drill, and after he settled in, Chloe took off on foot. The air had a bite when she stepped back outside, warning that winter wasn't far behind. Pulling her leather collar up, she started walking. From her online search of Jackson Hole, there were only a few motels in town besides the bed-and-breakfast. Several blocks away, she circled the first one, but there was no beige sedan. The car was parked right in front of room number 126 at the second motel.

Avoiding the security lights, Chloe stayed in the shadows and ducked to one side of the car. Rising, she peered through the windows, but there was nothing on the seats, front or back. In a crouched position, she ran to the door, then checked the room's single window. No light from a television or computer screen seeped past the edges of the curtains.

Hopefully, they were fast asleep. Taking a deep breath, she pulled a set of lock picks from the pocket of her leather pants and stood there, staring at them for the longest time. She thought of the people who would be disappointed if she broke the law. Stan, Sarah Rutledge and Uncle Henry. She'd walked on the straight and narrow ever since those harrowing teenage years, and she realized she couldn't do it.

So she wouldn't be tempted to change her mind, she tucked the tools away and hurried toward the sidewalk fronting the motel. Turning right toward the bed-and-breakfast, she slipped the knife from her sleeve and into her right hand as a large body moved silently from the woods hugging the sidewalk.

She stopped when she recognized the sheriff and flipped the weapon in the air before shoving it back up her sleeve. She disliked being caught off guard, surprised he'd slipped up on her. That's what she got for disregarding her own instinct for survival and not paying attention while agonizing over doing the right thing. Had he been in the woods the whole time? Had he seen her standing in front of room 126?

He stood close, his legs spread in an intimidating manner, but she refused to back away. That would reek of weakness. Best to go on the defensive. She looked up—way up—and moved even closer. She'd learned that nifty move while working with dogs. Always move forward and the dog would move back. It put the human in the pack leader position. Only problem was, Sheriff

Hoyt didn't react like her furry friends. He stood firm, as if *he* was at the top of the pecking order.

She rocked back on her heels and went for the casual approach. "Nice evening for a stroll, Sheriff."

He glanced at the motel, specifically toward room 126, before refocusing his attention on her. His big grin threw her off balance.

"It certainly is. How about I walk you back to your room? Jackson Hole is a relatively safe town, but we do get quite a few out-of-towners."

The night's excursion was shot anyway. Playing it cool was her best option.

"Fine by me."

In her peripheral vision, Chloe spied movement near the sedan sitting in front of room 126, but she kept her attention on the sheriff. Had the two men slipped out of their room while she wasn't looking? So as not to arouse suspicion, she turned and started walking. Sheriff Hoyt fell into step beside her. The fine hair at the nape of her neck prickled, and it wasn't because of the man walking next to her. She needed to shake off the sheriff and find out if the two men had left their room. She could double back and surprise them without breaking into their quarters. Nothing illegal in having a nice, friendly chat.

She aimed an arrow straight at his heart. "So who's keeping an eye on Penny while you're patrolling the streets?" She kept her tone friendly, but increased her pace. She'd duck inside the bed-and-breakfast, then slip out the back and hoof it back to the motel. She had to know if they were following her.

He didn't answer, and she stopped scanning their surroundings to look at him. She didn't care for the intent expression on his face and stopped in her tracks.

"What?"

He shook his head. "I can almost see your mind clicking a mile a minute." He faced her, and those emerald eyes bored into hers. Oh, yeah, the sheriff was definitely good at his chosen profession. "Miss Bailey, if you have a problem of some sort, I'm happy to help. You can trust me, you know."

She might be only twenty-five years old, but she'd had a lifetime of experience. There were only four people she had ever dared to trust. The sheriff appeared to be squeaky clean, but so did a lot of other people. People who were just better at hiding their dark sides.

She'd learned early on she had to look after number one. Even God hadn't been able to save her parents.

"I appreciate that, Sheriff, but I don't have any problems other than getting back to Mrs. Denton's. Geordie could probably use the bathroom about now."

She snapped her mouth shut, knowing she'd messed up before he even said anything.

"Please, call me Ethan. I have to ask myself why you didn't bring that cute little dog of yours along with you for your evening stroll."

Time to get rid of the sheriff. She had to make tracks back to the motel. "Sheriff Hoyt—Ethan—I appreciate the company, but rest assured, I have nothing to hide." And wasn't that the biggest whopper she'd ever told? "Tell Penny I said hello and I'll see you around town." But not if she could help it. Ethan Hoyt had good instincts, probably sharpened by his time spent as a detective in Chicago, but from the time she was sixteen, Chloe had been hanging around a gang of FBI agents. She could outwit him any day. Stan always grumbled that she had too much confidence, and one day it would land her in a boatload of trouble.

As she turned to leave, a bullet whizzed by close enough to slice the skin on her ear. It pinged into a car parked on the street behind her. Her survival instinct kicked in. She pivoted around and plowed into Sheriff Hoyt, throwing both on them onto the sidewalk, hopefully out of the line of fire. Her mind went into overdrive. They were out in the open, and whoever shot at her could easily have taken her out. Was it a warning shot, letting her know they were watching?

A big oomph shoved the breath from Ethan's lungs as Samantha Bailey pushed him to the ground and landed on top of him. Before he could catch his breath, she slid off his body and started belly-crawling toward a parked car on the street. Glancing over her shoulder, she hissed, "Get a move on. Someone just shot at us."

Stunned, impressed and somewhat put out by Miss Bailey's quick reflexes, he flipped himself over and followed her. He crouched beside her as she peered around the front end of the vehicle. Where had she learned moves like the one she'd performed after the gunshot?

She twisted her head around and he spotted a thin line of blood trickling from her earlobe. His body tensed, and he pulled his gun from his shoulder holster. "You're bleeding. Are you okay?"

She grinned and her dimples flashed. "I'm fine. They just nicked my ear." The grin disappeared. Her lips firmed, and the gold ring around her brown pupils burst into a brilliant golden fire. "But they'll wish they hadn't before this is over."

He briefly wondered about Miss Bailey's life.

Most of the women he knew would be close to hysteria after being shot at, but that was something he could think about later. Right now, he had to protect her, whether she thought she needed it or not.

"Move back. I need to get to the front of the car to see what's going on."

She hesitated a second, then shrugged her shoulders and scooted behind him. Ethan took a quick peek around the hood of the car but didn't see anything. Gun in hand, he dropped back behind the safety of the vehicle and leaned against the front fender.

"Did you see or hear anything, Sam?" He winced when she took a swipe at her ear with her coat sleeve, but the blood kept seeping out.

She squinted down the lane, lit only by streetlamps, then gave him a saucy grin. "We've been shot at together, so I guess we're friends now."

Her degree of calmness after getting shot at bothered him, but they were out in the open. Now wasn't the time to delve into Sam's life.

"Fine, we're friends now. Did you see or hear anything before the shot?"

He could almost see her mind sifting through different answers. It was a yes or no question. The woman was wily as a cat. His temper got the best of him. "It's a simple question. You shouldn't have to think it to death."

Her chin shot up and she wore a mulish expression. "Fine. Right before we walked away from the motel, I saw a shadow moving around the car in front of room 126."

"And you didn't see fit to tell me?" His voice echoed incredulous anger.

Her gaze shifted away. "I'm used to handling my own problems." She thrust her sweetly pointed chin forward. He had to bite back a grin. In some ways, Sam reminded him of Penny with her stubbornness.

"I'm sure you are, but I'm the sheriff and we'll do this my way. By now the shooter could have circled around us. We need to move."

Her eyes shifted toward the motel before they settled back on him. "I'm sure the shooter is long gone, but if you want to accompany me back to the bed-and-breakfast, I'd appreciate it."

He wasn't a fool. He knew exactly what the clever woman planned. "And after I drop you off, you're going to sneak out and come right back to the motel."

Her eyes widened and she dipped her chin. *Jackpot!*

"Admit it," he said.

"Seems to me you already know everything, Sheriff."

She smiled, but he didn't trust the sassy upturn of her lips. He might as well let her tag along while he checked out room 126. Maybe it would keep her safe and out of trouble. Later the two of them would have a nice long talk. He wanted to know what she was doing standing outside the room of two men from New York so late at night.

He heaved a heavy sigh. "I know you have a knife and a gun. I want to see the permit later, but for now, stay behind me and do exactly as I say, or I'll take you to Mrs. Denton's and lock you in your room while I check this out."

She flashed him a full-wattage smile, and her dimples made another appearance. She looked young and innocent, nothing close to the wily woman she had already proved herself to be.

"Sounds like a plan." She tilted her head. "You're a real by-the-book lawman, aren't you? It's all black-and-white for Sheriff Hoyt. No wiggle room for extenuating circumstances."

He harbored the uneasy feeling that her whole life revolved around "extenuating circumstances." "I told you to call me Ethan. We're not very formal here in Jackson Hole. Come on. Let's move quickly. We'll make our way down the street, using the cars for cover, and check out room 126. Stay close behind me," he added when she tried to slip past him.

She did as he asked and stayed behind him as they crouched behind cars and wound their way around the back of the motel. There was no sign of movement anywhere, so Ethan stepped in front of room 126. He raised his hand to knock, but Sam grabbed his arm, effectively stopping him.

"What now?" he muttered, pulling back his arm and facing her.

Exasperation covered her face. "You're just going to knock on their door? In the middle of the night?"

He raised a brow. "I'm the sheriff, Miss Bailey, and we were shot at. I have every right to investigate the situation."

She seemed to ponder that a moment. "Shouldn't you call for backup or something?"

He ignored her and rapped his knuckles against the wooden door. The room stayed quiet. He knocked louder this time. "This is Sheriff Hoyt. Open the door, please."

Nothing. Sam tried to nudge him out of the way.

"What are you doing?" She was fiddling with something in her hand and approached the door lock. He couldn't believe it. She was going to jimmy the lock. He grabbed the set of picklocks out of her hand.

"You can't break into a motel room. It's against the law." And then it dawned on him. Earlier, when she'd been standing at the door to room 126, she'd planned to break in. But why? He'd get answers later. Right now he had his hands full.

Her face scrunched into a scowl. "You are the law, and I'm with you. That makes it legal, right? Besides, you got a better idea, hotshot?"

They struggled a moment for possession of the picklocks, but brute strength gave him the advantage. The woman snarled at him like a rabid dog when he jerked them out of her hands.

"Yes, I have a better idea. I'll wake the manager and ask him to open the door."

That took the wind out of her sails.

"Fine, but I want my hardware back."

"I don't think so."

She scowled again. "Whatever. Let's get this show on the road."

It didn't take long to rouse the sleepy manager, and soon they were again standing in front of room 126. Ethan stepped in front of everyone and inserted the key. "Stay back." The manager had already moved away, but Sam was still breathing down his neck. The woman was like a barnacle.

Ethan turned the key and opened the door. The stench of blood assailed his nostrils. He pushed Sam backward. "This is a crime scene. I'm going in, but do not step past the threshold of this door." He moved forward but glanced around to see if she was obeying his orders. He was taken aback to see a look of shock, mixed with a healthy dose of fear, on her face.

It was an indication that Sam was in this thing up to her cute little ears. He decided then and there that the woman wasn't leaving his sight until he had some answers. He touched the wall until he felt the light switch. With a flick of his wrist, the room was bathed in light. Even without taking a pulse, there was no doubt. The two men he'd seen riding in the sedan were dead.

FOUR

The sickly smell of death hit Chloe smack in the face and she took a step back.

She'd helped Stan's FBI cyber unit on many cases, but computers were her area of expertise, not dead bodies. She'd never visited an actual crime scene.

Closing her eyes, she took a deep breath of clear, crisp mountain air and centered herself. A picture of Peter Norris rose in her mind, and she wondered if the same odor had permeated his office by the time they discovered his body.

She could see through the open doorway, and the sight of two men lying separately on two double beds, blood seeping from tiny holes in the front of each of their foreheads, was enough to make her want to toss her cookies. She took another deep breath and swallowed the bile rising in her throat.

Were the two men connected to the Peter Norris murder and her unidentified disc? She took another step back, away from the stench of death. She had to pick up Geordie and get out of Jackson Hole. She'd find a safe place to stay until she could figure this thing out. She turned to flee, but a strong grip on her arm stopped her.

"Don't even think about it, Sam."

Chloe schooled her face into a mask of calm as she spun to face Ethan. And when had she started thinking of him as Ethan instead of Sheriff Hoyt? "Excuse me? You told us to stay back."

His green eyes pierced her pretense. "You were getting ready to run, and I have several questions before you'll be allowed to leave town."

The shock of seeing the two dead men quickly receded and self-preservation took over. Something she had become very good at since the death of her parents when she was a child. "You have no right to hold me without just cause."

His rigid jaw tightened even more. "I have cause since I witnessed you standing in front of room 126. Fortunately for you, I followed you from the B and B. Otherwise, I'd be arresting you on murder charges. Give me your weapon." He held his hand out.

Panic constricted her throat. She didn't like feeling boxed in, not after her short stint in juvenile hall before Stan rescued and took custody of her, but she quickly regained her equilibrium. No way was she giving up her gun. She'd been shot at and these two New Yorkers were now dead. She had a burning desire to get out of town, and she'd need protection when she left.

Forcing herself to relax, she took a step back. "You're way off course, Sheriff Hoyt. As you said, you followed me from the B and B. I didn't have anything to do with this."

His hand stayed extended and his jaw looked hard as granite. She got the sinking feeling that she was now seeing the real Sheriff Hoyt, the hotshot Chicago detective Mrs. Denton had described.

"We won't have a time of death until the coroner arrives. You could have been revisiting the scene. Give me your weapon."

She had no choice, so, feeling as if she were giving away a part of herself, she pulled the gun out of her jacket pocket and handed it over, butt first. It was an insult when he shook out a handkerchief and took her weapon, but then another thought sent a second panic wave roaring through her. Her prints were on the gun, and she had no doubt he'd run them through the system. Her prints were on file with the FBI because anyone who worked there was fingerprinted as part of their policy.

Chloe quickly reassured herself that he wouldn't find anything from her past, only her real name. He shouldn't be able to get into her juvenile record unless he had a valid reason to present to a judge. But even knowing her real name would be problematic. He'd want to know why she'd given him an alias. That would lead to questions she didn't want to answer. She had to get out of there and away from Jackson Hole as soon as possible.

Her handkerchief-bound Bersa disappeared into his jacket pocket, and she was already thinking of a way to retrieve it when his voice caught her attention.

"Don't even think about it, Sam. I'll return your weapon after we get some answers."

She shrugged, trying for nonchalance, but inside she shivered. "Whatever. I'm in the clear because I had nothing to do with this—" she lifted her chin in false bravado "—and you can tell yourself you know what I'm thinking, but you're wrong."

Ethan stared at her hard, but a squad car pulled into the parking lot and gained his attention. She was vastly relieved by the interruption. He must have been an ace detective, because he stood there looking all righteous and dignified, silently urging her to spill her secrets, daring her to do the right thing. The man had probably never even had a parking ticket.

A young, clean-cut guy dressed in a starched

police uniform hurriedly got out of the patrol car and rushed toward Ethan.

"Sir, I got here as quick as I could."

And when, exactly, had Sheriff Hoyt called his deputy? Almost as if he could hear her thoughts, he turned his head toward her. "I texted my deputy to come as soon as I saw the bodies." It shocked her that he could read her so well, but she covered her surprise by holding up her hands. "Did I say anything?" It came out sounding waspish, but she was in a waspish mood. Things were going downhill fast. Ethan motioned his deputy into the motel room, but not before he gave her instructions. The kind of instructions she didn't like.

"Stay put. Don't make me come after you."

Her gut was screaming at her to run as fast as she could, but the good sheriff had her picklocks, her gun and, worst of all, her prints.

She crossed her arms over her chest. "Fine."

He gave her one last hard look and disappeared into the room. Thirty minutes later several vehicles pulled up. One man got out of a car carrying a medical bag. She assumed it was the medical examiner. Two men exited the second car carrying an array of cases. They looked like crime scene techs. A few minutes later, Sheriff Hoyt stepped out of the room with a hard jaw and a purposeful stride. He took her by the arm and she jerked it back. She'd give it one last shot.

"I want my picklocks and firearm returned. I haven't done anything wrong."

He just stood there, looking all grim and tough. Well, she wasn't in a good mood, either, and jerked the tiger's tail. She shouldn't have, given the situation, but couldn't seem to stop herself. She gave him a saucy grin. "I had to try."

He didn't look amused, and the grin slid off her face as the gravity of the situation hit her. She ran a hand through her short hair.

"It's late and I'll give you two options. We can go back to the bed-and-breakfast and make a nice big pot of coffee for our little informative chat, or we can have bad coffee at the station and spend our time in the interrogation room. Your choice."

Another shiver racked her body at the thought of being in a police station, so she chose wisely, but didn't give in easily. "Fine, we'll go to the bed-and-breakfast, but you're going to have to apologize when you catch whoever—" she waved a hand toward room 126 "—did this."

Silence shrouded the patrol car as Ethan drove them to the B and B. He hadn't taken the time to run the plate numbers he'd collected earlier, but that was fast becoming a priority. He had a bad feeling that Sam was in this thing up to her eyeballs.

Sam stared out the window during the short drive. The coroner had offered to give his deputy a ride home. He and Sam could have walked, but after getting shot at and finding two men dead in the motel room, he didn't feel it was safe, and that angered him. They had their minor incidents, but Jackson Hole had always been a safe town. Now he had a double homicide to solve.

He parked the car on the side of the street in front of the B and B and cut the engine. He didn't acknowledge Sam as he dug his cell phone out of his pocket. He hit speed dial, and the babysitter answered on the third ring.

"Margaret, this is Ethan. I'm sorry to call so late, but I'm going to be tied up awhile."

"Is it true? Did you find two dead bodies in the motel?"

He sighed. Jackson Hole was a small town, and he should've known the happenings at the motel would spread like wildfire. "Yes, you heard right. There were two murders at the motel. Listen, can you take care of Penny the rest of the night? And could you swing by my house and pack her enough clothes for several days and bring her to the B and B in the morning? I'll see that she gets to school. Oh, and pack me a few changes of clothes, if you have time. I sure would appreciate it."

"Sure thing, Sheriff."

"Thanks, and make sure everything is locked up tight before you turn in. Don't worry, I'll be careful. Bye."

He hung up the phone, lowered his head against the headrest and closed his eyes. The close call with Sam getting shot in her earlobe, then seeing the two dead men, brought death to the forefront of his mind and stirred memories of his deceased wife. He and Penny had finally found a measure of peace after the long, cruel terminal disease had taken Sherri's life. He'd hoped his small family would thrive and be happy in Jackson Hole, but Sherri, being a city girl, had never quite fit in with the small-town folks. It wasn't that she thought she was better than the town's people—she just didn't fit in, no matter how hard she tried.

A sharp voice intruded into his thoughts. "Margaret your girlfriend?"

He opened his eyes, the memories drifting away, and turned his head. He stared at the woman sitting in the passenger seat of the patrol car, a woman his gut was telling him had brought a truckload of trouble with her to Jackson Hole. The first woman since Sherri died who had even remotely caught his interest, not that he'd follow up on it. He wasn't interested in finding a wife, and even if he was, he didn't want another city gal, especially one who rode a Harley, had guns and knives stashed on her person, and owned an attack poodle. "Not that it's any of your business, but Margaret is my babysitter."

Her next question volleyed right on the heels of his answer. Sam was a spitfire. "You going somewhere?"

It took a minute for him to remember she'd heard him speaking to Margaret on the phone. He took grim satisfaction in answering her. "Penny and I will be temporarily staying at the B and B until I can sort things out and get some answers."

Her right eye twitched, but she kept her expression neutral. At such a young age, Ethan wondered where Sam had acquired skills that took most detectives years to learn. Hiding your emotions was hard to accomplish, which made him all the more curious about her past.

"Why were you following me in the first place? You had no right to do that."

Deflecting attention away from yourself was another highly coveted skill, one that Sam had learned well.

He shifted in his seat and turned toward her. "I don't have to give you an explanation. Now, do we have our chat here at the B and B, or do we go to the station?"

She fingered her right cuff with her left hand, and he wanted to kick himself for forgetting about the knife she had hidden up her sleeve. She immediately relaxed her fingers when she caught him staring and grabbed the door handle. He thought about taking the knife from her, but let it go for the moment.

"Fine, let's get this over with, because I'm shaking this town's dust off my feet as soon as possible."

He grabbed his own door handle. "Fine with me." And it *was* fine with him. He didn't like being even remotely attracted to a woman shrouded in secrets. He had enough to deal with trying to raise his daughter. But he had to admit he was curious about Sam, and he was determined to get some answers. Back at the motel, he'd slipped her gun to his deputy and instructed him to put a rush on running the prints. He'd know soon enough if Sam was in the system.

Mrs. Denton had given Sam a key, and it was very late when they entered the foyer. He had just stepped over the threshold when she whipped around to face him.

"I have to check on Geordie before we get started. He probably needs to go to the bathroom."

He folded his hands across his chest. "Fine, but make it fast."

A glimmer of annoyance appeared in her eyes before she patted his arm and released her inner Southern charm. "Don't you worry none, I'll be back in a jiff."

He watched her agile leather-clad body take the stairs two at a time. She reminded him of a cat burglar, which was not a comforting thought. He moved into the kitchen and discovered Mrs. Denton, bless her heart, had left a pot of coffee already made.

He knew where everything was from having spent a good deal of his childhood stopping by to nab cookies on his way home from school, so he pulled down two mugs. The cream and sugar followed. He was getting ready to pour coffee into the mugs when Sam rounded the door frame of the kitchen with her poodle wrapped tightly in her arms. He froze when he saw the expression on her face. She was trying to hide it but failed to suppress the underlying fear.

He put the coffeepot back where it belonged and rounded the kitchen island to stand in front of her. "Sam, what is it?"

She finally looked at him, as if just realizing he was standing there, and shook her head. "Somebody's been in my room. They went through my things."

It didn't take but a few seconds for the information to register, and his heart pounded at the implications. "Mrs. Denton," he breathed. If anything, her face paled even more, in stark contrast to her short black hair.

"No," she whispered, then louder, "no!"

She turned and raced toward the stairs before he could get in front of her. He grabbed her arm on the top step and pulled her back. "Wait," he whispered forcefully. "You wait here while I check out her bedroom."

She nodded and he removed his gun from his jacket pocket. After one last look to make sure she stayed put, he crept down the hallway and stopped in front of Mrs. Denton's room. He pressed his ear to the door, but didn't hear anything. Slowly, he eased the door open and saw the older woman tucked into bed. Nothing looked disturbed, and he breathed a sigh of relief when he heard gentle snoring. The perpetrators were probably long gone. He closed the door and nodded at Sam. Her shoulders sagged in relief, and he was glad to see she cared about Mrs. Denton's safety. Taking her by the arm, he led her farther down the hall. He wanted to check out her room. They were about halfway there when the fur ball in Sam's arms released a low, fierce growl.

Ethan stopped walking and looked at Sam

for direction. He didn't know what the growl meant, but he saw fear, mixed with a healthy dose of courage, on her face and watched the knife slip from her sleeve and into her hand. He tensed a second before a closet door to his right slammed open with maximum force. The impact of the door caught him in his right side and he stumbled before falling to the floor. He caught a glimpse of a masked man jumping out of the closet, gun in hand, and knew they were in trouble, and in that moment, he was glad he hadn't confiscated Sam's knife.

FIVE

Chloe assessed the situation in an instant and knew that if shots were fired someone might get hurt. She gave Geordie a sharp command, dropped the dog to the floor and, a split second later, released the knife already balanced on the edge of her fingertips.

It flew past Ethan, who was reaching inside his jacket to retrieve the gun she knew he kept there, and embedded itself in the upper arm of the masked gunman. Mean dark eyes glared at her from the holes in the ski mask, and the guy shook Geordie's teeth off his ankle before he fled down the hallway. Ethan scrambled up off the floor and turned to pursue, yelling over his shoulder, "Lock the doors behind me and take care of Mrs. Denton."

Chloe picked up Geordie and held him close. She was shaken by the surprise attack, but the assault itself only hastened her urge to flee. It was like a living thing in her body, something she'd battled her whole life. When life got dicey, she ran.

Geordie whimpered in her arms and licked her on the chin. She kissed the top of his soft head and glanced toward Mrs. Denton's room. As badly as she wanted to throw her stuff in a duffel bag and get out of Jackson Hole, she couldn't leave a defenseless old lady alone with a gunman on the loose.

She heard the front door slam. Her window of opportunity to flee closed as Ethan's heavy footsteps pounded up the stairs. His dark hair appeared first, followed by flashing green eyes.

"I thought I told you to lock the door behind me." His bellow was loud enough to wake the dead, but his belligerence helped her to get rid of the shakes. She could deal with this far better than the mess her life had become.

"I decided it was safer to stay close to Mrs. Denton's room. What if there had been two of them? You need to give me my gun back, and now I'm going to have to buy a new knife." She tried to sound nonchalant, and she succeeded, judging by the look on his face. She wasn't nearly as blasé as she let on, but she'd spent years learning to mask her emotions. First at juvenile hall, and then at the FBI.

He took a deep breath, as if reaching for a fountain of patience, and took several steps past her. "Let's have a look at your room, then you and I are going to have a nice long chat."

As she followed him down the hall and into her room, her stomach roiled and her mind worked frantically to separate what she could say that would pacify him long enough for her to leave town. She was a master at doling out half-truths. Not lies, just not the full truth. Sarah Rutledge's sweet, radiant face swam into her mind, reminding her that half-truths were the same as lies, but Chloe highly doubted that Sarah had ever had a killer nipping at her heels.

If the room toss was connected to the murder, were they searching for the mysterious disc? Ethan studied the room with those eagle eyes of his and, as if echoing her thoughts, said exactly what she was thinking. "Unless you find something missing, it looks to me as if someone was searching for something." Storm-filled eyes, backed up by well over six feet of toned muscle, turned in her direction. "You know of any reason someone would want to go through your things and shoot at you, Sam?"

She studied the room while avoiding his sharp, intelligent gaze boring a hole through her skull, as if trying to forcefully extract the answers he wanted. Her duffel bag had been upended in the middle of the beautiful handcrafted blanket covering the bed, and her toiletries were scattered alongside the few clothes she'd packed. The blanket had been thrown back, and the pillows tossed to the floor, but all in all it wasn't too big a mess. Maybe they were looking for identification to confirm they had followed the right person since she'd used a fake name.

As if she'd be stupid enough to leave her information anywhere but on her person. Identity theft was a big international problem, and she knew how to protect herself, online and off. Stealing identities was for the novice hackers. Her skills went far beyond that.

In her arms, Geordie gave a happy bark right before Mrs. Denton rounded the doorway of the room. Her nightgown was one of those old-fashioned numbers with lace on the collar. Her pink bedroom slippers looked ancient.

She lifted a hand in the air. "I heard a ruckus going on in the hall, but it took me a few minutes to find my Taser. It was in the bathroom. Must've forgot to put it on my nightstand."

Ethan's tight lips softened and his taut jaw relaxed when he looked at Mrs. Denton. Chloe wondered if he'd ever look at her like that, then castigated herself. It didn't matter how he looked at her. She needed to get out of Jackson Hole so people like Mrs. Denton wouldn't get hurt because of her.

While giving the older woman a quiet, condensed version of events, Ethan started herding Mrs. Denton out of Chloe's bedroom, but glanced over his shoulder. "The kitchen in five minutes. We need to talk. And don't even try to leave. I'll come after you."

They disappeared, and Chloe plopped down on the bed with her dog still in her arms. She rubbed her cheek against his soft brown curls. "Why does trouble always have to follow me, Geordie? Why can't I just be a normal person like everyone else?"

She got a lick on the chin, then she placed her most trusted companion on the floor. She had only a few minutes to get her facts lined up, at least the facts she was willing to share with a man of the law.

After assuring Mrs. Denton he had everything under control, Ethan closed the door to her bedroom and took a deep, calming breath before starting down the stairs. Sam was an enigma. He shuddered at the thought of being even remotely drawn to a woman who seemed to attract trouble like flies at a picnic. Then those dimples of hers would make an appearance and his heart would almost stop. And she just had to be kind to older ladies like Mrs. Denton. That made it worse. Ethan had a real soft spot for elderly people.

Just because she was the first woman to catch his eye since Sherri had died didn't mean he had to do anything about it. It was probably nothing, just a passing fancy—an attraction to the odd and unusual—because he certainly hadn't ever met anyone like Sam. Plus, the woman was in some kind of trouble, and it was his job to dig out the truth.

He wanted answers, and he intended to get them. He'd been a top-notch detective in Chicago, based on the number of cases he solved, and he'd dust off his old skills and get to the bottom of this mess.

He entered the kitchen, ready to pry the answers out of her, and stopped short when she looked up from the coffee mug she was cradling with both hands and smiled at him. Those two cute little dimples popped out on her pixie face, making her look like the most innocent person alive. He didn't trust her sudden friendliness. Slowing his steps, he moved to the counter and poured himself a cup of coffee while planning his line of questioning.

She beat him to the punch and attempted to take control of the interview.

"Listen, Sheriff Hoyt," she said, and tilted her head to the side and widened her smile. "Sorry, you told me to call you Ethan. I know you want answers, and I'd love to help, but I don't know anything that would help solve any of the events that have recently occurred."

She looked relaxed, even sounded relaxed, but her right hand tightly gripping the coffee mug gave her away. The lady was nervous and he intended to use that. He sat down across from her and leaned back in his chair. After taking a sip of coffee, he placed the mug lightly on the table.

He softened his tone, made it almost cajoling. "I understand, but anything you can think of that could help will be most appreciated. I have two murdered men, a shooting and a break-in to solve." He leaned forward with what he hoped was an earnest expression on his face. "I have a town full of citizens and tourists to protect, not to mention my own daughter and Mrs. Denton."

The dimples disappeared, her lips formed a thin line and the ring of gold around her pupils burst into fire. "You need to brush up on your psychology classes, Sheriff. The best in the business have tried to figure me out and come up with zilch."

Bingo! His first clue. Sam, at some point in her life, had had professional counseling. "Would you care to elaborate on that?"

He saw the moment she realized her mistake. She stiffened, then relaxed, grinned and leaned back in her chair. "You're good."

"So they tell me." It wasn't bragging; it was

fact. He'd always been assigned the toughest cases in Chicago and had had a high rate of convictions.

She rubbed a finger around the rim of her mug, and he knew she was trying to figure out how much she could tell him while keeping herself in the clear. He'd done this hundreds of times and could practically predict how a perp would react. Not that he considered Sam a perp, but he was positive she was at the center of everything that had happened.

She surprised him with her next statement.

"My real name is Chloe Spencer." She kept her gaze on the coffee mug when she dropped her bombshell but lifted her eyes, full of the earnestness he had projected earlier. It was almost as if she was throwing his psychology manipulation back in his face. "And I witnessed a murder, but that's all I'm going to tell you, because I'm afraid for my life. That's why I used an alias."

Chloe. He rolled the name around on his tongue. It fit her better than Samantha. Then he realized the corner she'd neatly boxed him into.

"You knew I'd find out your real name because I have your prints on the gun I confiscated, and the tag number off your motorcycle. You've just given yourself a convenient excuse for not telling me about the murder you witnessed because you're afraid." He couldn't believe she'd outsmarted him. Was any of it even true? He knew her name was real because that could be checked, but what about the rest?

"Where did you witness this murder?" When she stayed quiet, he brought out the big guns. "Well, no matter, we'll get to the truth soon enough, and you're not going anywhere until I have some answers."

That little piece of news broke her silence. She shot from her chair and started pacing the floor. Geordie whimpered, but she ignored him. Finally she turned on him, and for the first time he was certain she was telling the truth. "Listen, Ethan, this has nothing to do with you, and if I leave town, all my problems will follow me. Your town, the tourists, your daughter and Mrs. Denton will be safe."

She stood in front of him, her eyes filled with the truth of her statement. With the exception of her giving him a fake name, the majority of the time he was able to sort the truth from lies, and Chloe Spencer was telling the truth. Armed with this knowledge, he took another long look at the woman. Running seemed to come naturally to her. Had she done a lot of it in her life? Was there anyone who cared enough to help her?

Well, he was going to help her whether she liked it or not; plus, he had three crimes to solve.

The murder, the break-in and the fact that some-one had shot at them.

"No."

"No? Did you say no?"

He saw her absently fingering her right sleeve with her left hand and was thankful her knife had left the premises embedded in the perpetra-tor, which reminded him. "That's what I said, and just where did you learn all those nifty moves with a knife?"

She looked over his head, as if remembering something in her past, then looked down and gave him a saucy grin. "Wouldn't you like to know?"

Ethan shoved to his feet. She didn't seem the least bit afraid. He had some calls to make to get a description—even though it wasn't much of one—of the perp out on the wire. Maybe the guy would go to an emergency room for the knife wound.

"It's not long until daylight. I suggest you get some sleep."

She called her dog to her side and strolled to-ward the doorway.

"Oh, and Chloe, don't think of sneaking out. I'll be in the room beside yours, and I'm a very light sleeper. Ask Penny." He paused. "I'm going to find out why you were standing in front of room 126 tonight."

She shot him a disgruntled look and disappeared with her dog trotting at her side.

Ethan grinned, even though he had a big mess on his hands. He hadn't felt this alive since before Sherri died. Maybe even longer than that.

SIX

Tension filled Chloe's shoulders the second she stepped into her room. Geordie hopped onto the bed and she plopped down beside him. What to do? Her inclination was to run, but to where? She couldn't go to Stan and Betty's. That was the first place the killer would look.

She also didn't want to see disappointment on Stan's face because here she was, once again, in the middle of a mess. Chloe had never figured out why they'd taken her in when she brought so much trouble. She'd always assumed the judge had contacted Stan when he'd realized the extent of her hacking skills and wanted her to use her talent—and teach her a valuable lesson—by helping people at the FBI. Not long after that, Stan and Betty had asked if they could adopt her. She had been so happy she hadn't asked any questions. She'd assumed they wanted her because they didn't have any children and she and Stan had so much in common with their computer skills.

She was a street tough kid, but they never gave up on her. And Stan was bossy, but he had a big marshmallow heart.

She ran her hand through her dog's dark curls. "Whatcha think, Geordie? Stay and hope there are no more incidents until we find the disc, or hit the road?"

On the one hand, she was safe here with Ethan dogging her heels, but what if someone got hurt because of her? She couldn't live with herself if Penny or Mrs. Denton were injured, or worse. She didn't like to think of Ethan getting hurt, either.

Her stomach rumbled, reminding her she hadn't eaten much of anything that day. She was tempted to go downstairs and raid the kitchen, but she didn't want to run into Ethan if he had the same idea. She couldn't handle another interrogation at the moment. Ethan was good at his chosen profession. She hadn't made a slip like the one she made earlier in years.

Exhaustion caused her shoulders to slump forward as the reality of the attack in the hall sank in. The guy who killed Peter Norris had somehow tracked her to Jackson Hole. She thought of all the precautions she'd taken and couldn't figure out how they'd found her. She'd been careful, but they must have had a man on the ground at her apartment and followed her to Jackson Hole.

She rubbed her temples where a slight headache had started and decided to stay in Jackson Hole, at least for one more night. She needed to rest and come up with a plan. Geordie had already scratched himself out a place on the bed to sleep. Dragging her feet, she went to the bathroom, changed into the old T-shirt she slept in and brushed her teeth.

After her parents died, she'd learned to shut down her brain when she needed sleep. It was a habit that came in handy now. She slumbered almost as soon as her head hit the pillow, her last thought on the burner phones she'd hidden in Geordie's pouch on her Harley. She was glad she'd had the forethought to do that since the person who'd tossed her room had strewn her stuff on the bed for all to see, all being Sheriff Hoyt. As sleep overtook her, she made a mental note to get in touch with Stan the next morning.

Never a morning person, Chloe grunted and cracked one eye open when her bed shook for the second time. Geordie growled playfully, and a squeal of delight accompanied the doggie snorts of happiness. It was too early in the morning for anyone in their right mind to be that happy, and she had a good idea who was in her bed playing with her dog.

Without rolling over, she grumbled, "Are you supposed to be in my room?"

The bed stilled, and Chloe flipped onto her back. Ethan's precocious daughter looked bright and shiny as a new penny—no pun intended—in her cute jeans and frilly top. The mulish downturn of her lips ruined the cutesy effect.

"My dad says we have to stay here at Mrs. Denton's because you're in trouble, but I can put up with you because I get to play with your dog and eat chocolate chip cookies." Chloe curled her lips in anticipation. The kid reminded her a little of her own young, feisty self.

"Tell you what," Chloe dramatized with a Southern accent, "you can play with Geordie when you learn some manners."

It didn't surprise her when Penny's lower lip trembled and a big fat tear rolled down her cheek.

Chloe snickered. "Is that the best you've got? That might work on your daddy, but I know better."

Sure enough, the waterworks dried up real quick, only to be replaced by a challenging glint in Penny's eye. Let the games begin.

"Penny," Ethan's voice roared down the hallway, "you better get back here this instant."

Chloe pulled the covers to her chin just as he rounded the corner of her doorway, a door that Miss Penny Hoyt had left wide open.

He skidded to a stop, his eagle eyes missing nothing as he scanned the room. His gaze finally landed on Chloe tucked under the covers, his daughter sprawled on the bed, and Chloe's dog salivating over said daughter.

Staring at father and daughter, Chloe's stomach cramped at the thought of this small family getting hurt due to her precarious situation. Penny had already lost her mother, and the kid would be distraught without her father. Chloe knew what it was like to be without both her parents.

"It's too dangerous for her to stay here. What if we have a repeat of last night?"

That caught Ethan's attention and his gaze locked onto her. "Mrs. Denton's Bed-and-Breakfast will be the safest place in town by lunchtime."

She squirmed in bed. This probably wasn't the best time to be having a serious discussion. "How so?"

"Because I'm letting it be known that Penny and I will be staying here for a while, and I plan to leave a patrol car parked out front day and night."

She chewed that over for a second. "That might work."

He shot her a tolerant grin. "I have been known to come up with a good idea or two over the years."

"Well, didn't that just put me in my place."

"Daddy, she just sassed you. That deserves a time-out."

Chloe couldn't let that one go. "So you know all about time-outs, do you?" Penny's cute little face clouded and turned red, but Ethan stepped in.

"Penny, it's time for breakfast and then school. I'll drop you off this morning."

His statement brought the seriousness of the situation back to Chloe. He was dropping his daughter off at school because there was a possible killer out there, waiting to get his hands on Chloe. The urge to flee pounded in her skull.

"And you, Chloe, will be coming with us. You'll spend the day at the station with me."

His unwavering gaze made her decision. She'd accompany him and grab a burner phone from Geordie's bag on the Harley on her way out so she could touch base with Stan and Betty. She didn't have a plan, and this would give her time to come up with something.

"Okay," she acquiesced, and he shot her a suspicious look before herding his daughter out of the room.

After disappearing, he called, "Make it fast, Chloe, or Penny will be late for school."

She threw back the covers and grumbled out loud about his tone—she wasn't a six-year-old—and Geordie grunted when he hopped off the bed.

They'd left the dog happily chomping down on one of Mrs. Denton's cookies, and Ethan had just dropped Penny off at school. He glanced at the woman sitting stiffly and staring out the passenger window of his patrol car. Today she had on skinny jeans and a sweatshirt with a picture of her mutt on the front. He didn't miss much, and he'd seen the tightening of her hands before she crawled into his car.

"You're uncomfortable around law enforcement. Feel like sharing?"

She tensed, then relaxed before turning and gracing him with a saucy grin. "Why, Sheriff, there you go pulling out that imaginary psychology degree again." She batted her non-mascaraed lashes. Sherri would never have been caught outside of the house without a full face of makeup, but as far as he could tell, Chloe hadn't bothered with any. Not that it mattered. She had beautiful porcelain skin.

He gripped the steering wheel. He couldn't determine why the woman upset his equilibrium, and he shouldn't be thinking about her skin. She would be out of their lives as soon as he solved the layered mysteries surrounding her, and solve them he would.

"I have your number, Chloe. You turn sarcastic when you're upset, and you're upset right now, so let's cut to the chase. Why don't you tell me everything you know and we'll get some answers?"

That wiped the fake smile off her face. She started chewing a nail and he felt like a jerk. Maybe her hard-core exterior hid a terrified woman inside and she really was scared for her life.

"You know, I bet a really good lawyer could get me out of Jackson Hole in a heartbeat. I haven't done anything wrong and you have no right to keep me here." That ruined his assessment that she might actually be like a normal woman, scared witless under the circumstances. On the other hand, at least he didn't have to deal with any hysterics.

He turned into the station parking lot, pulled into his reserved space and turned off the engine. He twisted toward her and discovered he was right. Not a scared bone in that lean, athletic, cat burglar body. Her eyes held defiance.

"You're forgetting one thing. I saw you standing in front of that motel room where two men were found dead, and you're not going anywhere until I have some answers, so get used to it."

She snorted, sounding much like her dog, and he hid a grin as he opened his car door. She scrambled after him but hesitated when he held the front door to the station open for her.

"Don't like police stations, do we?"

She lifted her sculpted chin and stepped slowly through the door.

Wanda waved at him from the dispatcher's desk and he headed that way. She handed him a stack of messages and strained her neck to see who was behind him. While sifting through the notes, he moved to the side so she could see. "Wanda, this is Chloe Spencer. Chloe, Wanda Armstrong. Wanda is our dispatcher and all-around office person."

Wanda gave Chloe a big smile and immediately started her interrogation, down-home style.

"Well, hello there. It's nice to meetcha. You just visiting Jackson Hole, or are you and the sheriff good friends?"

Ethan had no time for this, and he didn't want to give the gossip mill anything to feed on. "I'm helping Miss Spencer with a few problems she has, and there's no reason anyone in this town should know about it." He followed that statement with a hard stare. Wanda got the message loud and clear.

"Now, Sheriff, you know I'm as discreet as they come." Wanda included Chloe. "You need to talk, Miss Spencer, you let me know. I'm a good listener."

Chloe nodded and Ethan decided she really was uncomfortable in a police station. He made his way to his office in the back, trying to figure out how to use that to his advantage.

He seated himself behind his desk and Chloe followed, but she didn't sit down. She wandered around his office, first staring at his certificates and commendations hanging on the wall, then moving on to the framed pictures he had placed on a small shelf. She had her back to him.

"Is this Penny's mother? The one Mrs. Denton told me about?"

He should be past all that by now, but he swallowed the lump in his throat. He knew every detail of the picture she was looking at. He'd stared at it for days after Sherri died. "Yes." His answer was clipped, but he didn't want to discuss his deceased wife.

"Do you believe in God, Sheriff Hoyt?"

That question caught him by surprise. In the short time he'd known her, Chloe never failed to surprise him.

"Yes, I believe in God. I go to church most Sundays, too."

She turned, and he was taken aback by the fierce look on her face. "Good for you." It was the first time Ethan had seen real emotion on her face. Not the persona she had developed to show the world. Had something happened to make her disbelieve?

"And you, Chloe," he asked softly, "do you believe in God?"

The tension left her body, and she sat down and slouched in the seat facing his desk. The coy smile he was coming to detest curved her lips. "Sorry, I didn't mean to get personal. I need to buy a laptop. Is there anywhere in town I can purchase one?"

He let her momentary lapse go. For now. "There's a computer store in town. I'll take you there after I catch up on my messages."

"I appreciate it. I need to check on my email and stuff."

"Did you forget to pack your laptop when you fled the scene?"

She snapped her head up, then lifted a finger and waggled it in the air. "No-go, Sheriff. Better men than you have tried to trip me up." She stood. "I'll leave you to catch up on your work. I'll just wander around the station for a while."

"Stay in the building. Don't make me come after you."

"Wouldn't dream of it."

She walked toward his office door and was almost run over by David Cummins, his young, overly energetic deputy.

"David, watch where you're going. You almost knocked Miss Spencer down."

David was growing into his gangly body and had a touch of peach fuzz on his face that he liked to think of as a beard in progress. He almost stumbled in his haste to apologize to Chloe.

"I'm sorry, it's just that I have something important to show the sheriff."

Chloe waved him forward, and David almost stumbled again in an attempt to show Ethan a picture that had come in over the wire. "Sheriff, this just came over the fax machine. It probably has nothing to do with us, but I wanted to show you right away."

Ethan took the picture from David, wondering if he'd ever been as excited, or as green, as his deputy. "Thanks, David. I'll look it over."

"Sir, the feds are all over this one. Some hotshot CEO of an international tech company was murdered. His name is Peter Norris."

If he hadn't been looking up, Ethan would have missed Chloe's face going pasty white as she grabbed onto the door frame for support. This was it. This was the murder she had witnessed.

He came out of his chair and walked toward her. "Chloe, is there something you'd like to share?"

SEVEN

She was busted. Maybe. She could still salvage this. Ridding herself of the visuals playing in her head of Peter Norris lying dead in his office, she went for casual but failed, even to her own ears. "I don't know what you're talking about, Sheriff. How would I know anything about a big CEO's murder?"

Ethan looked thunderous and she flinched under his hard stare. He kept his gaze on her as he spoke to his deputy. "David, have you run the prints on the gun I gave you at the motel murder scene?"

"Yes, sir," he said crisply, then scratched his head. "Come to think of it, the name that came through is the same as Miss Spencer's here." He cast Chloe an accusing look. "Is that your gun?"

She'd had enough of this. She hadn't done anything wrong, and she didn't deserve to be stared at by Ethan's deputy like a criminal. She lifted her chin and took a step toward the young guy. "You bet it's my gun, and I want it back if you're finished with it."

She received only a moment's satisfaction when David Cummins took a step back, which made her feel like she'd just kicked a puppy, but she couldn't believe she'd dropped her guard and let Ethan see the truth in her face.

"David, I need to talk to Miss Spencer. Close the door on your way out."

David shot her a satisfied look, as if she'd been called to the principal's office, and made himself scarce. As soon as the door closed, Ethan sat down behind his desk and pointed at the chair in front of it.

"Sit."

Chloe slid into the chair, her mind working furiously, figuring every angle. She could tell Ethan everything, but then she'd be putting Stan and Betty's lives at an even higher risk, and she wasn't ready to do that. She needed to handle this herself. On the other hand, she had to find that disc, and if she didn't, keeping Ethan in the dark wouldn't be an issue because she might not live long enough for it to be a problem.

He leaned back in his chair, looking all relaxed, but keen intelligence shone out of his eyes, eyes that were focused on their target, which would be her.

"I can have David run your name and find out

everything about you. Eventually, I'll discover the truth. It would be better for you, in the long run, to volunteer the information."

She'd never figured out how she ended up in these types of messes, but here she was, once again.

His chair creaked when he leaned forward and propped his elbows on his desk. "Chloe, I can help if you'll let me."

She didn't doubt that, but for some odd reason she didn't want to see disappointment on his face if he ever found out about her past.

"Before we start, I need to make a phone call." She had a burner phone in her jacket pocket—the one she'd swiped from Geordie's pouch on the Harley after telling Ethan she had to grab something before loading up in the car that morning—and she needed to check in with Stan. That would buy her some time to come up with a plan and check in with her adoptive parents at the same time.

She slipped out of her chair, wanting to run for the door, but forced herself to walk. "I'll be back in a minute."

She half expected him to hold her hostage in his office, but he didn't say a word when she closed the door behind her. She snagged one of the hard plastic chairs lining one wall and tugged the phone out of her pocket, goose bumps prickling her arms. Police stations gave her the willies.

She punched in Stan's private cell number—a secure phone that was less likely to be bugged—and it was answered on the first ring. "Chloe?"

There was a sense of urgency in his voice, and she got a bad feeling that things were about to go south. Still, she played it cool in case her imagination was working overtime.

"Yeah, it's me. I just wanted to check in—"

"Chloe, I want you to shut up and listen."

"But—"

"Listen." His voice sounded gruff—full of love mixed with authority—much the same as it had when he'd gotten her released from juvenile hall by taking full custody of her when she was sixteen years old.

"Okay." She chewed on her thumbnail, something she hadn't done since she was a kid.

"The police department forwarded the FBI cyber unit an anonymous email sent to them, asking us to track down the source after their own department failed to do so. The email stated that CEO Peter Norris had been killed in his office late one night. Chloe, there was no body found at the scene."

She couldn't stop the harsh intake of breath that paralyzed her body. No body? "But—"

"I said listen." The words were harsh, but she

knew Stan, and she detected the underlying fear mixed with frustration.

Her blood ran cold. "Okay."

He took a deep breath. "I received your email about going on vacation, but when I couldn't reach you on your cell phone, we got worried and Betty and I decided to drop by your apartment." His voice lowered. "Chloe, Peter Norris's dead body was in your apartment when we arrived. I noticed that your computer was missing, and I know you never go anywhere without it. I didn't know where you were and couldn't reach you, so I called the police when I discovered the body. The examiners already know he wasn't murdered on-site, in your apartment, but they want to talk to you. As a favor, I asked them to give me a few days to bring you in, so they delayed putting anything out on the wire. You have to come home as soon as possible so we can get this straightened out. I know you're innocent. I have faith in you. Please come home so we can prove you weren't involved in this."

Chloe wanted to cry, but she hadn't cried since her parents had been murdered on the mission field. She couldn't cry because she was afraid that if she started, she'd never stop. Stan hadn't asked if she was innocent, and his blind trust in her had her swallowing a lump in her throat.

"Stan, I had nothing to do with this. I'm an

innocent bystander, but you and I both know, with my unflattering past, they'll lock me up until I'm proven innocent."

She started shaking at the thought of being in a jail cell. She couldn't let that happen, even for a short while.

"Chloe, I know your first instinct is to run, but in this case that's a very bad idea."

She had to get off the phone and make plans. She had to find that disc.

"Stan, everything will be fine." She glanced toward Ethan's office. "I know a very good detective who will be glad to help me figure this out." At least she hoped he would. "I'll check in and let you know I'm okay. Please don't worry and give Betty a kiss for me."

She ended the call and sat there for a few minutes, taking in this new turn of events. Her quicksilver mind came to a horrifying conclusion. This was another way for the killer to put pressure on her to give him the disc. It would also be a nice and tidy closure of a high-profile case that the police and FBI could wrap up quickly and present to the public as a job well done. The killer thought he could pin the murder on her. She knew exactly how everything would go down, but she wouldn't allow that to happen.

* * *

Ethan glanced up from the messages he'd been trying to concentrate on and stared at his closed office door while waiting for Chloe to finish her phone call. He was more curious than he wanted to admit about who she was calling. Boyfriend? Partner in crime?

His curiosity spiked, and his trouble antennae waved a big fat red flag when the door was flung wide open and she stood on the threshold, determination stamped across her face.

Briskly she strode to the chair in front of his desk and lowered herself, sitting on the edge of the seat. He waited, even though he had a dozen questions, but she didn't leave him hanging for long.

"There's been a few developments and I need some help."

He leaned back in his chair, assuming a false sense of relaxation. Funny how her long Southern vowels had turned brisk and short. "Is that so?"

She winced as she lifted her chin, which only accentuated her secretive pixie face.

"Yes, that's so." She leaned back in her chair and mimicked his air of calmness. "But we're going to have to make a deal before I divulge any information."

The red flag started flapping furiously in the breeze as he leaned forward, propping his elbows on his desk, all business now. "If you've committed a crime, I won't make any deals, but if you need my protection in connection to witnessing a crime, I'll help you."

Her pupils widened for a fraction of a second, which was enough to tell him she might not reveal the whole truth. He gave her a hard look and she shifted in her seat. Another telling sign of discomfort.

She lifted her chin and looked him in the eye. "I didn't have anything to do with Peter Norris's murder." Her eyes darted to the right before settling back on him. A sure sign she was, at the very least, not telling him everything.

"I'm pretty good on a computer. I have clients who pay me to test their company's cybersecurity. Sci-Fi Works Corporation is one of those businesses. One of their board members suspected someone at the company of selling client lists to the highest bidder.

"I set it up so I would be notified if someone opened their system late at night, and I was watching for any aberrations during working hours. Peter Norris logged on to his computer late on the evening of his murder." Her words sped up, as if she wanted to get it all out as quickly as possible. "I opened the portal to the webcam, and he was sitting at his desk when I looked. Someone knocked on his door while the camera was still operating. Peter Norris got up and answered the door, but I couldn't see anything at that point. Someone came in, but I couldn't hear what they said. The next thing I knew, a gun appeared on-screen and a shot was fired." She shivered, and Ethan decided her reaction wasn't fabricated.

"There was blood spatter on his webcam." She swallowed hard. "The shooter got in front of the camera, where he knew I could see him—he wore a ski mask—and he said that, yes, Peter Norris was dead, and that he'd been looking for me for a long time. He told me the delay had cost him a lot of time and money and that I had to give the disc to his deliveryman, who would be at my door any minute." The words came even faster now. "I had to get out of there. I have no idea what he wants. I don't have a disc of any value. I needed time to figure out what he wanted, and I didn't care to meet up with his 'deliveryman,' so Geordie and I packed up and took off. He must have somehow tracked me down and set the whole thing up at Sci-Fi Works to frighten me into giving him what he wants."

Ethan didn't doubt that she'd witnessed the murder, and he had a lot of questions.

"You don't know what the killer is referring to in relation to the disc?"

She shook her head with an answering no, but he wasn't sure he believed her.

"That's just it." Her voice was filled with frustration. "Why didn't he just explain about this mysterious disc?"

"There's a lot of holes in your story."

Her pointed chin lifted and belligerence laced her words. "Like what?"

"Like why you didn't call the police. Why run?"

She started chewing on her thumbnail but slapped her hand on her thigh when she realized what she was doing. "I'm a woman alone and I didn't trust the police to protect me."

Ethan chuckled. "Lady, I've seen the arsenal you carry around. And let's not forget your attack dog. Try again."

The gold rimming her brown eyes shot fire at being called out, but he got what he wanted.

"Fine, but I want a deal. I can prove everything I just told you. I hit the record button on my computer, which automatically saves everything in the cloud, as soon as I heard an argument between Peter Norris and the killer. And I also recorded myself as a security measure that protects me in case there's ever any question what I'm doing. The time stamp and location of the device proves I wasn't anywhere in the vicinity of the murder. You can keep me in your custody while we find out who's behind this, because I'm not turning myself in as a witness while my life is in jeopardy. We'll have to go to New York."

Ethan's mind raced as he processed the information. He had to admit he was intrigued by Chloe and the information she'd just laid out. He loved being sheriff in Jackson Hole, but it had been a long time since his heart had beat with the excitement and thrill of an intriguing case.

"New York is out of my jurisdiction."

She tilted her head and her eyes gleamed. "If you refuse to help me, I'll run, and trust me, this time no one will find me."

Ethan didn't like being backed into a corner, but he liked the thought of Chloe being harmed even less. The killers had likely tracked her to Jackson Hole—if the incidents that had happened in his town were connected—and it was a good bet they would find her again.

"Tell you what… Level with me and I'll consider it."

She crossed her arms over her chest and the leather creaked. "No way. I want your word that you won't call the authorities until we figure out who killed Peter Norris. Otherwise, I'll run."

Her stubborn chin told the tale. She meant

what she said. He really didn't have any choice unless he wanted to officially detain her, and he didn't have enough evidence to warrant that. If he didn't agree, he had no doubt she'd slip out of Jackson Hole and he'd never see her again, but he wasn't going to make it easy on her, not when he was possibly risking his career over this.

"I have two murders to solve that may be directly connected to the Peter Norris killing. Fine, I give you my word that I won't contact the authorities unless we uncover information instrumental to the case. Now it's time for you to fess up. Why didn't you call the police when you witnessed the murder?"

Her eyes flashed with irritation. "As I told you, I was checking into a situation for a board member. That's private and confidential information. The killer also threatened someone I love, but this goes way beyond that. I have to find out about this disc he wants, and if I call in the authorities, they'll be all over me like a swarm of angry yellow jackets.

"You already promised you wouldn't contact the authorities unless there was information instrumental to the case." She took a deep breath. "There's more."

"More?"

"That phone call I made earlier?"

That was his next question, who she'd called. "I'm listening."

"Well, I couldn't just leave Peter Norris's body to be found the next morning by his coworkers, so I sent the police an anonymous email. I routed it through a bunch of servers so it would take several days to trace it to the internet café in New York where I stopped before coming to Jackson Hole. It gave me time to leave town and I made it to Jackson Hole after three days of hard riding. The phone call I made a few minutes ago was to an FBI guy I know. He said Peter Norris's body was found in my apartment."

After dropping that bombshell, she sat still as a statue, allowing him to absorb that startling piece of information before she started speaking again.

"He stated that the examiners have already determined the body had been moved there after, you know, his death, but they want to talk to me." She leaned forward, all earnest now. "Ethan, I need your help. I have to find out about this disc, and you know there's a lot of pressure on the authorities to wrap up a case as quickly as possible. You know what that means."

He did. On several of his big cases in Chicago, he'd been under scrutiny from the public and the media, but he'd ignored them and done the job. Some investigators were pushed into getting a conviction as quickly as possible and mistakes were made along the way.

"I need to see the video before we go any further."

"What kind of system do you have here at the station? I had to leave my laptop and smart phone behind because they could be tracked and I didn't want to wipe the hard drive. The FBI guy said my laptop was missing when they found the body in my apartment."

"How do you know this FBI guy, and what made him notice your laptop was missing?"

Her thumbnail flew to her mouth, but her hand stopped midair, and she slowly laid it back on her thigh.

Gotcha.

EIGHT

Chloe was expending way too much energy trying to stay one step ahead of Ethan.

"He's an acquaintance. I presume the killer removed my laptop under the assumption that I might have recorded the murder."

His chair creaked when he leaned back. It reminded her of the way Stan's chair had sounded when she was a scared, rebellious sixteen-year-old, sitting in a hard chair in front of his desk while he grilled her about the hacking job she'd done on the bank's computer system.

She reminded herself that she was an upstanding citizen now and she didn't have to take any guff from Sheriff Hoyt.

"You didn't answer my question. Exactly how are you acquainted with this FBI agent?"

"That information isn't instrumental to the case," she deadpanned.

He gave her a hard stare. "Fine. I don't know

what kind of computer system we have. How are you going to show me the video on my computer?"

Chloe relaxed. This was her area of expertise. "As I said earlier, I store everything in a secure hybrid cloud, protected by a virtual firewall. I also have detective control. That means when I access my cloud, I will be notified if anyone has slipped in the back door and retrieved my information."

A dark brow lifted over one piercing green eye. "I'll take your word for it."

He opened the laptop sitting on his desk and slid it toward her. She cracked her knuckles before placing her fingers on the keyboard. Ethan grunted at her antics, but she ignored him.

"Okay, your operating system is Windows 10." She tapped the keys rapidly. "I see you're on a multiuser system?"

She looked up and caught the blank look on his face. She got that a lot from people who had only basic computer skills. "You're connected to other computers here at the station?"

He nodded, and she smiled to herself. The good sheriff was used to being in full control, and his lack of computer knowledge didn't seem to sit well with him.

"I'm checking to make sure no one has slipped in the back door and messed with my stuff."

Chloe blew out a sigh of relief. "I'm accessing my cloud and no one has hacked in. Both videos should be safely stored, but just in case, do you have a thumb drive I can back everything up on?"

He pulled a drawer open and handed her a thumb drive. Chloe checked the storage data. "This should work." She stuck it into a USB port and hit the download button.

"It should only take a few minutes to—" Chloe sat straight up in her chair and her fingers frantically hit the keyboard. "Oh no, you don't, you slimy toad. You're not stealing a copy of my files."

"What? What's going on?"

Ethan's voice barely penetrated her brain. "Be quiet! I need to concentrate."

Chloe was in the heat of a cyber battle with an unknown. It didn't take but a few seconds to realize the person who had followed her through the door she opened to her cloud wasn't deleting her information, just copying it. But why? And how?

She used every trick she knew—and she knew almost all of them—to stop the person, but nothing worked. Whoever was in her system was just as computer savvy as she was, maybe even more so, and that was very impressive. The download and copy was completed simultaneously and she went on the attack. "Come on, come on, come on." She chased the worm back through the system and was able to attach a worm of her own before it disappeared into cyberspace.

She flopped back in her chair and stared at her computer screen. Unbelievable. No one ever got the drop on her. She was that good. It wasn't bragging, it was just fact.

"What happened?"

It took Chloe a few seconds to refocus. "Someone piggybacked me into my cloud and copied my files." She looked up. "That means someone else out there has a copy of the murder video."

"Will the person who stole your computer have a copy, too?" Ethan asked.

"Let's just say I have good security on my computer. It's possible, but highly unlikely."

"So what about the person piggybacking in your cloud?"

She gave him a saucy grin. "I tagged his tail. Let's see if we can find our little thief."

She downloaded a program, put in her password and opened it up. Within seconds a screen popped up and she watched her worm traveling across a map of the United States, then it went international. She released a long whistle.

"Whoever slipped into my cloud is good. Better than good."

"You sound impressed," Ethan said from across the desk.

Her eyes stayed on the screen as her worm hit server after server. "I am. Not many people in the world could have accomplished what this person is doing. I've matched computer skills with the best, and no one has come close to this person."

Chloe wanted to kick herself for accidentally revealing that little piece of information. She didn't expect Ethan to miss her slip and he didn't let her down, but she really wished he would have.

"And where did you match computer skills with all these people?"

She looked him in the eye and fell back on her old standby. "That's not relevant to the investigation."

Ethan closed his eyes. She didn't doubt it was in frustration, but she didn't care to reveal her life story to the man.

"When am I going to see the video?" Yep, Ethan definitely had a little frustration thing going.

She checked the path of the worm and scooted to the edge of her seat, shocked at what she was seeing. "Ethan, do you know of any computer whizzes who live in Jackson Hole? Because the tracker I placed on the worm is headed straight back here. Unless..."

"Unless?"

She looked up. "Unless this person is so good they're sending my worm back to me." She slid the laptop sideways so he could watch. The red dot had returned to the United States and was making its way back to Wyoming. Although it didn't return to her computer, it finally stopped at a place not far from them. Chloe enlarged the map and pointed at the stationary blinking red dot.

"The person who slipped into my cloud is there, at least their computer is there. Of course, this could have been done remotely."

Ethan leaned forward and stared at the map. "Well, I'll be. That's Ned's mountain."

"Who's Ned and what do you know about him?"

His furrowed brows indicated he wasn't happy with the situation.

"Ned showed up in Jackson Hole about three years ago, bought a mountain a mile or so from here and built a cabin. He comes into town for supplies and that's about the only time anyone ever sees him."

"I can run a search. What's his last name?"

The wrinkles between his eyebrows scrunched up even more and Chloe almost laughed. The sheriff wasn't a happy camper.

"I don't know his last name. He's never caused any trouble and keeps to himself. On occasion he even finds lost hikers in the mountains and brings them back to town."

"Do you know the address on the mountain?"

"No."

"No problem. I'll check the records at the courthouse and see who purchased the property."

"Fine, go ahead, and then I want to see that video."

She pulled up the Jackson Hole courthouse website, and Ethan gave her the name of the road leading up Ned's mountain. He didn't know the street number, but when she looked at the records, it didn't matter. The land mass was huge and there was only one name on record on that road. She laughed.

"What's so funny?" And didn't the sheriff sound grumpy.

"Well?" Impatience had edged into his voice and Chloe bit back a grin.

"The person—or company, I should say—recorded as buying Ned's mountain is RBTL."

"That makes no sense. Don't they have to give their full names to buy property? And what does RBTL stand for?"

Chloe's lips curled at the edges. "It's ingenious, really. In computer slang, RBTL stands for 'Read Between the Lines.'"

* * *

Ethan absorbed this new piece of information. Ned had never broken the law or given Ethan cause to look into his life, but now they needed to have a little chat. He wasn't sure if Ned had broken any laws, but then again he didn't understand computers.

He looked at Chloe. "How did Ned, or this person, follow you into your cloud?"

Pulling the laptop closer to her, she started typing at an impressive speed. A few minutes later she looked up and her dimples appeared when she smiled. "Good thinking, Ethan. Ned, or whoever is on the mountain, planted a worm at some point so the police station's computers could be monitored." She grinned even wider. "Ned, or someone, has access to everything coming into the station via computer. That's against the law, you know."

Horror filled him at the thought of someone spying on police business. Maybe it was time he found out more about Ned.

It also seemed to him that Miss Spencer knew an awful lot about the law. "Yes, it is."

She frowned, and he got a bad feeling. "What now?"

"Well, it's possible that someone else routed everything through Ned's computer so it would appear to come from his server."

Ethan felt a headache coming on. Give him a solid homicide any day over this computer mess. He knew how to work email, and get on the police sites, but anything more than that was beyond his capabilities.

"Let's take a look at the video, then I'll pay a call on Ned before we go any further."

"We'll pay a call."

"What?"

"You said it yourself. You don't know squat about computers. You might need my help."

The tiny hammers working at his temples increased in rhythm.

"Fine, you can accompany me to Ned's. Pull up the video. Let's see what you've got."

Ethan wasn't really worried about Chloe going with him up the mountain. From the small amount of time he'd been around the mountain man, he had never sensed any bad vibes. The guy just wanted his privacy. But then again, if Ned was actually spying on the police station's computers, that would change things.

Chloe did some fast typing on the laptop and turned it around for him to see. Neither one of them said a word as he watched it in its entirety. He also watched the second video where Chloe taped herself. When it ended, he leaned back in his chair and tented his fingers.

"Well?"

Her voice held anxiety. He didn't know if she was telling him everything, and she was a computer expert. He wasn't, but he was a quick learner and he had picked up some things in the last few minutes.

"Could your computer have recorded this remotely?" The person threatening Chloe on the video was a man, but he knew pictures and videos could be doctored.

She snarled, sounding a little bit like her poodle, tapped a series of keys on the laptop and pointed at the screen. "That's why I record myself. You can see my apartment in the background, so the location of the device can be verified. See the clock on the wall behind me? I placed it there for a reason. The second hand is moving, proving I'm at that location, present tense. In my line of business, it pays to protect myself."

Ethan bit back a grin. The anxiousness in her voice had been replaced by righteous indignation. He believed her, but he tried to reason with her one more time. "I still don't understand why you don't want to go to the police or FBI, and who is Stan? The killer mentioned him in the video."

She shrugged. "He's just someone I know, and you're forgetting about the body being found in my apartment, even though they know Peter

Norris wasn't killed there." She lifted a defiant chin. "Are you sticking to the deal, or not?"

Ethan sighed. She'd run if he didn't do it her way—and probably get herself killed in the process.

"I'm sticking to the deal." He stood and grabbed his jacket off the back of his chair. "Come on, let's pay a visit to Ned, and then we'll swing by the school and pick up Penny."

Instead of exiting at the front of the station, Ethan led Chloe from his office, down the hall and out the back door.

"What are we doing back here?"

Ethan pointed at a red Jeep parked in the rear entrance along with two other cars. "We're taking my personal vehicle. It's better suited to mountainous roads and terrain. I keep it here for these types of occasions."

She grinned. "That's a cool ride. Not as nice as my Harley, but a close second."

Ethan shook his head as they climbed in. Chloe was in a class of her own, but he did like her spunk.

The engine roared to life and he pulled out of the parking lot and into the street. "It shouldn't take over thirty minutes to get there."

She grunted a response and he glanced at her profile while she stared out the window. What was it about this woman that intrigued him? She was the complete opposite of Sherri. She was feisty with a healthy dose of self-confidence.

Not that he would do anything about the temporary attraction. He had a daughter to raise, and he hadn't done the best job of being a husband the first time around. Plus, Chloe Spencer had secrets.

Ethan looked ahead through the car window. He always felt like a speck of dirt under the towering old-growth pine trees when he visited one of the mountains in the area. He also felt God's presence more vividly in the wilderness.

Chloe's rear bounced off the seat and she mumbled something under her breath when he hit a particularly deep rut.

"You call this a road? It looks more like a ravine to me."

Ethan grinned. "I guess a city girl like yourself isn't used to roughing it."

She snorted. "I know all about roughing it. You'd be surprised at some of the places I've been to."

He jumped on that opening. "Tell me."

He glanced at her and felt bad at seeing the blood drain from her face, and then she shrugged.

"You have my real name now and can find out anything you want to know." She looked at the passing scenery. "I grew up in North Carolina. My parents were missionaries and were killed on the mission field. I was ten at the time. I spent six years in an orphanage before I found a home. End of story."

The Jeep hit another rut and he almost lost control of the vehicle. After using brute strength to guide the Jeep back onto the road, he thought about what Chloe had said—and hadn't said. There was anger mixed with frustration and a deep hurt she tried to hide during the short, nonchalant recap of her life. Was it her parents' deaths on the mission field that caused her to ask if he believed in God? Had she lost her faith?

The cabin came into view and he tabled his thoughts. He could process this new information about Chloe later. Right now he needed to interview Ned. He unbuckled his seat belt.

"Stay in the car while I approach the cabin."

She chuckled. "Unsure of your welcome?"

The woman was sassy. "Just stay put while I check things out."

She threw up her hands. "Fine, I'll play the little woman and hide out in the car."

Ethan chuckled. He couldn't help himself, and he was smiling when he opened the door. He noticed his bootlace was untied and bent down to tie it just as a bullet whizzed over the top of his head. He jerked upright and twisted back into the seat, slamming the door behind him. "Get down! Get down!"

NINE

Chloe bent over, her head almost in her lap. "Was that what I think it was?" She couldn't believe someone had gotten the drop on them again. "This is starting to tick me off."

Ethan turned his head, a look of absolute disbelief written on his face. "Is that all you have to say? What kind of a life have you led that someone shooting at you doesn't upset you?" He shook his head. "Never mind. We have to get into the cabin. I'm going to start the engine and drive as close to the porch as I can. I think the bullet came from above us and to the left. The porch is on the opposite side. We should be safe enough."

Chloe ignored his outburst and grabbed her door handle as Ethan peeked over the steering wheel and drove the Jeep right up to the porch steps and cut the engine. He pulled a gun out of his jacket pocket.

"Okay, you go first. Open the door and run.

We're on the side away from the shooter, but I'll cover you."

"What if the door is locked?"

"I was up here once before to check on Ned during a blizzard. He doesn't have a lock on his door."

She shot him a saucy grin and he frowned. She enjoyed keeping him off balance. "Okay, here we go." Chloe took a deep breath, flung the car door wide, ran up two steps and pulled the front door open. Placing her body behind the safety of the door, she peeked around the side and watched Ethan slide to the passenger seat and exit the passenger door. In seconds, he ran past her and slammed the door shut behind them.

"Stay away from the windows."

"Duh, like I don't have enough sense to do that." He gave her a look similar to the ones he gave Penny when he was exasperated. She really didn't mean to sound snarky, but his comment about her life ticked her off. She should apologize, but he moved through the cabin, checking the two rooms.

Chloe took in her surroundings. It wasn't much to look at. Log walls. A tiny kitchen/living area, a bed pushed against the wall, and one small bathroom with a privacy door. What struck her was the neatness of the place. It made her think of military precision.

Avoiding the two windows, one on each side of the cabin, she wandered around the small space. There wasn't much to see. An old couch with a ratty afghan folded across the back. A coffee table, but no side tables. No computers or television anywhere, not even a smartphone or tablet. A mountainous landscape on one wall, pretty high-end. Being a lover of the arts, Chloe squinted at the signature at the right-hand bottom of the painting. The name Ned was scrawled in tiny letters. No last initial. She filed away that small piece of information—you never knew when it might come in handy—and focused on Ethan. She checked out the gun in his hand as he stood to the side of the kitchen window—the one facing the shooter side of the cabin—and kept watch.

"I didn't know an S&W was standard police issue."

He glanced back at her. "We have more of a choice now. I like the feel of the S&W M&P 9. It works for me. You know a lot about guns."

She ignored his snoopy, unspoken question. "As soon as we return to town, I want my gun back. I need it now. We just got shot at again."

Ethan ignored her complaint and glanced at the opposite window. "Keep a watch out that window, but stay to the side and be careful. I'm pretty sure the shot was long-range, and in all probability the guy has fled, but we still don't know where Ned is."

Now she really wished she had her gun, her knife and her dog. She didn't doubt that Mrs. Denton was spoiling Geordie. "You think Ned shot at us?"

"Ned's been in Jackson Hole awhile, but no one really knows much about him. I'm not taking any chances."

Chloe felt a small draft coming from the ceiling and glanced up. She froze in her tracks when she realized she was staring at the bad end of what looked like an AK-47. The man staring down at them through the hatch in the roof was scary looking, deadly scary.

Was this the man after her? If it was, she and Ethan were sitting ducks, and she didn't have a weapon on her anywhere. If they made it out of this alive, she was going to get her gun back even if she had to steal it from the police department lockbox.

"Huh," a gruff voice said from above. The caveman tossed his weapon in the direction of Ethan and the sheriff caught it with his left hand, but Ethan kept his handgun pointed toward the bear of a man who dropped through the opening. His feet hit the floor with barely a whisper, and Chloe took a step back when she got a good look at him.

He had to be at least six-and-a-half feet tall. Frizzy hair covered his face, but intelligent green eyes took her measure. He wore holey, faded jeans and a heavy fleece jacket. The man was huge.

"Ned," Ethan said.

"Sheriff," Ned responded.

Now that she was pretty sure she wasn't going to be shot, Chloe regained her equilibrium. "Talk about men of few words," she mumbled to herself, and both men turned toward her. No one was shooting, so she might as well get the show on the road. At the rate they were going, it'd take Ned and Ethan all day to communicate.

"Listen, Ned, someone just shot at us. You know anything about that?"

A bushy brown eyebrow lifted and Ned just stared at her for a second. Chloe would rather have fled to the tiny bathroom, away from that intense stare, but she stood her ground.

"Huh," Ned repeated.

Ethan stepped in. "Ned, we came here to talk to you and someone shot at us long range from the east side of the mountain. Do you know anything about that?"

Ned pointed at the weapon he'd tossed Ethan. "Check it."

Ethan kept his gun in his hand and laid Ned's weapon on the floor. He studied it, rose to his feet and tucked his own gun back inside his jacket pocket.

"It hasn't been fired recently. Ned, did you see the shooter?"

Ned's chin dipped in answer. "Was tracking him on the ridge. Found his spot right after he left. Didn't go after him because someone, you, entered my cabin. He's gone."

Chloe swiveled her head around, taking a close look at the walls and the ceiling. There were no signs of security anywhere. No cameras, no wires, no trip alarm that she could see. How did he know they'd entered his cabin? But, really, that wasn't important right now, and Chloe had had enough.

"Do you have a computer here?"

Ned's eyes flickered the tiniest bit before he turned to Ethan. "I keep to myself and bother no one." He waved a hand at the one-room cabin. "You see a computer?"

Ethan shook his head. "No, I don't see a computer."

Ned stared at them until Ethan backed off. "Let me know if you come across any information on the shooter." He turned as he took Chloe by the arm. "And I'll be back if I find out that you've been spying on the station's computers." He pulled her forward. "Let's go."

She pulled her arm away. "That's it? He didn't really answer the question. It was an evasion."

Ethan stopped on the threshold of the door. "I don't have a warrant and I have to take the man at his word."

What a waste of time. She couldn't believe Ethan wasn't pushing Ned harder.

Ethan left her standing there as he headed toward the car, but she stilled when a fuzzy whisker tickled her ear. "Your laptop is in North Carolina. Mocksville, to be precise. I'm sure you know how to find it. And tell Stan that Ned sends his regards."

Unlike his previous caveman speech, the cultured voice made Chloe freeze, her feet glued to the wide-planked floor. Ned knew Stan? FBI Director of Criminal Cyber, Response and Services Branch and her adoptive father? He must have seen her name on the station's computer system when Ethan ran her prints and checked her out. Ned had to be responsible for the worm in the system. Without looking back, she flew to the car, jerked open the passenger door and climbed inside, shaken to the core.

Ethan's mind was crowded with questions. He glanced at Chloe. She'd been quiet on the bumpy ride down the mountain. He almost missed her sass. Almost. The lady was an enigma, and he was determined to uncover all her secrets.

"Could someone have gotten into my computer and listened to our conversation and that's how they got to Ned's mountain ahead of us?"

Her face paled, and that made his stomach churn.

"It's illegal, but possible for someone to break into a computer with video capability and listen in on conversations. I was concentrating on my cloud. I caught the worm coming in, but I wasn't really paying attention to anything else at the time."

His fingers tightened on the steering wheel. "Great, now I have to worry about worms and someone listening to private conversations."

She chuckled, and it lifted his spirits. "I'll check it later, see if I can follow anyone's footprints in the system."

"Listen, I didn't push the issue with Ned because it was obvious he wasn't going to tell us anything and I didn't have a warrant to search the place."

He glanced at her. She had her thumbnail in her mouth, chewing away. As soon as she saw him looking at her, she jerked her hand down and laid it on her thigh. "I have to buy a laptop and then I'm going to North Carolina, with or without you."

"Why?"

"Before we left, Ned whispered something in my ear. He told me my laptop is in North Carolina. I should have already tried to track it." Her voice wobbled. "I know someone in North Carolina. I hope the killer isn't aware of them." She took a deep breath and faced him full on. "I told you the worm came from Ned's cabin and I was right. Very few people know how to track devices and Ned had already found my laptop. He must have copied all the information I have stored in my cloud and now has access to my laptop."

Chloe sounded cagey to Ethan. There was something she wasn't telling him.

"Did he say anything else?"

She averted her face, a sure sign of someone hiding something. "Not really."

He let it go for the moment. "Okay, how did he track your laptop to North Carolina, or do I want to know?"

The tension eased in the Jeep and she chuckled. "I'll tell you anyway. Most people aren't computer savvy. I installed a remote tracking and recovery program. If the thief doesn't wipe the system or disable the tracking program, and he boots the computer and connects to the internet, I can control the computer and track it."

It took a moment for Ethan to process what

she said, and when he realized the implication, excitement coursed through him.

"You mean there's the possibility we can track your laptop, and possibly the killer, through technology?"

She gave him a sideways glance and grinned. "Unless the killer gave it to someone else in order to throw us off his track."

"Great." Ethan knew he sounded disgruntled, but he couldn't help it. Chloe Spencer had shown up in Jackson Hole with a big attitude, a bag full of secrets, and a dog that would lick you one minute and bite you the next.

On the other hand, he hadn't felt this alive since his wife died.

"Fine, we'll get you a laptop and see if we can pick up the trail. If we can, we'll head to North Carolina. We don't have any other leads."

Chloe went quiet again, but he could only imagine the wheels turning at the speed of light in that agile brain of hers.

Out of the blue, she said, "Tell me about Sherri. Mrs. Denton said she died not long after you moved to Jackson Hole."

He didn't really care to talk about his past, but maybe it would encourage Chloe to tell him about her life. "*Back* to Jackson Hole. I grew up here but moved to Chicago after college. The Chicago Police Department recruited me right out of school. I worked my way up quickly and ended up in the Detective Division. I met Sherri, we got married and had Penny. I talked her into moving back to Jackson Hole because I thought it would be a safer and more wholesome place for our daughter to grow up."

"But?"

His hands tightened on the steering wheel. "But Sherri wasn't happy. She was a city girl. She tried to fit in, but it seemed like everything she did went wrong."

In a wry tone, Chloe gave her version of the events. "Bottom line, you blame yourself, and you're stoically raising your daughter while steering clear of any romantic entanglements."

Fury tore through him. "You don't know anything about it."

She snorted. He was laying his heart on a platter and the woman snorted.

"I know you're being selfish. Think about this. Maybe Sherri wasn't that happy in Jackson Hole, but maybe, just maybe, she loved you and her daughter enough that she was giving it her best shot, and had she not passed away, maybe things would have worked out."

Chloe's words hit him like a sledgehammer. Was it possible things would have worked out for Sherri in Jackson Hole, given enough time? He didn't know, and he didn't want to think about it right now. Time for Chloe to give up something.

"So what about you? You said your parents died on the mission field. That's an admirable choice of career. Helping others."

"Yeah, they helped others, all right," she mumbled under her breath.

Ethan heard her response and was surprised. "You didn't like them being in the mission field?"

She swung her head around just as the Jeep hit a particularly deep rut, but he caught the fierce expression on her face. "They died, Ethan. They were murdered while 'helping' people."

There was a swell of emotion in her statement and he decided to change the subject. The dirt road ended, and he turned the Jeep back toward town.

"You told me you have an apartment in New York and you own a company that helps corporations with their computer security. How did you get into that field?"

She shrugged. "It was a logical career, considering my computer skills."

Ethan was certain there was more to the story, but he let it slide for now. He pulled the Jeep into a space in front of the computer store and Chloe hopped out of the car as soon as it stopped. "I'll be back in thirty minutes." She disappeared into the store.

Before she got out of the car, Ethan had scanned the area for possible shooters and now took his first full breath since Chloe Spencer had blown into town. He pulled his phone from his breast pocket. It was one of those new smartphones that he barely knew how to operate, and he wondered if anyone out there was listening in or watching him through the camera lens.

He shook his head in frustration. Chloe had made him paranoid and he refused to live that way. He called the station and got his deputy on the line. Then again, maybe it would be prudent to watch what he said on an open cell phone line.

Earlier that morning, he had sent a text to David, instructing him to do a search on Chloe. He felt a little guilty, but wiped away those emotions—he had two murders to solve. She had admitted herself that a dead body had been found in her apartment, but she hadn't explained, to his satisfaction, enough about the person who gave her that information.

His gut was telling him Chloe was innocent, but he had learned not to completely trust his instincts, because look at what had happened when he'd moved his family from Chicago to Jackson Hole.

David answered on the third ring. "Cummins here."

"David, what did you find out about Chloe Spencer?"

"Well, Miss Spencer has led an interesting life, I'll give her that."

Ethan's patience was running thin.

"Information only, David."

"Yes, sir. Sorry. Chloe Spencer is twenty-five years old and she's an only child. She grew up in North Carolina. Her parents were killed on the mission field in Somalia when she was ten years old. There were no known relatives, so she was placed in the care of an orphanage in North Carolina until she was sixteen. Then all of a sudden she was adopted. It's unusual for someone that age to get adopted." Ethan gave a small growl and David hurried on. "Anyway, she owns a company called Spencer Security. The company is successful and the woman is fairly well-off. One interesting thing, though, is that her adoption was closed. The records are sealed, and I couldn't find out who adopted her."

Ethan was curious about her adoptive parents and why they had taken in an older child. He also wondered if Chloe and Peter Norris had had more than a business relationship. That would explain why the killer had chosen Peter as the first victim. The thought didn't sit well with Ethan.

"Is that all?"

"That's it."

Chloe stepped out of the store and Ethan closed the conversation. "Call me if you find anything else."

Ethan liked to gather all the information available. Sometimes small bits of information played into a case, and sometimes they didn't. Looking pleased with herself and carrying a large box and two small ones in her hands, Chloe climbed into the Jeep.

Ethan slipped the phone inside his jacket pocket.

TEN

When Chloe slid into the passenger seat of the Jeep, she was curious about the perplexed look on Ethan's face, but she was so happy to have her own technology in her hands that she ignored it.

He stared at the boxes she'd laid on her lap and she shrugged. "I withdrew enough cash before I left New York for any kind of emergency so the killer couldn't track me. I bought a smartphone and tablet along with the laptop. I can access my cloud from any device. I bought internet usage for all three devices, so I don't have to depend on Wi-Fi."

He nodded and started up the car. "I have to pick up Penny. School's about out for the day."

Chloe nodded and tore into the boxes. They'd removed them in the store to do the initial setup, but she needed to do some major tweaking on the devices to bring them up to her standards. She also had to download all her programs and contacts. She really needed to check her email.

There were bound to be more emails in her inbox than she wanted to deal with at the moment. And she was going to shore up the security on her cloud and email account so no one could tell if she accessed either.

"Can the killer track you on this new computer?"

She grinned. "Unlikely. I purchased it using a fictional name. But if anyone hacks into my cloud, they'll be able to track me. I'll divert my emails to my alias." Hopefully, all the precautions would buy her some time.

Ethan frowned as he pulled the Jeep into a parking space just as a loud bell rang and a slew of kids swarmed out the front door of the building.

Disapproval was written all over his face, and Chloe wished she'd kept her mouth shut about using a fictional name. Time for a big distraction. "How many kids can they fit into that building?"

Ethan sent her one of his distinctive interrogatory looks and she knew she'd slipped up. She huffed, "I was such a handful, they decided to homeschool me at the orphanage," and that was all of her past she was willing to share.

Ethan shook his head and got out of the car. Chloe ignored him and slipped the laptop out of its box and opened it up. Pure ambrosia. She laid her fingers on the keys, ready to get to work, but lifted her head and stared through the windshield. A blond-haired, blue-eyed streak of lightning peeled away from the mass of students and threw herself into Ethan's arms. Ethan hugged his daughter fiercely and turned in a circle, Penny laughing the whole time.

Chloe felt a deep pain grip her heart. Long-buried memories of her own father swinging her through the air rushed to the surface. She shook her head to dislodge the painful thoughts. Those memories were best left forgotten.

Ethan was opening the rear door, lifting Penny in, giving Chloe time to mask any emotion. She pasted a smile on her face and twisted around. "Good day at school?"

Penny scrunched up her nose. "What are you doing in my dad's car?"

The kid wasn't exactly rolling out the welcome mat, but Chloe was fast developing a soft spot for Ethan's daughter. Chloe pulled the tablet out of its box and held it up where Penny could scc.

"Look what I just bought." She didn't know if Penny had better computer skills than her dad, but most kids these days had a device in their hands practically before they could walk.

Her answer came when Penny leaned forward and tried to grab it out of her hand. Ethan had settled himself in the driver's seat and reprimanded his daughter while starting the engine and backing out of the parking space.

"Penny! You don't grab. If you would like to see something, you ask nicely."

Penny's lower lip trembled. Chloe shook her head as if saying, *That won't work on me*, and Penny's lip protruded in resentment. Chloe hadn't been around many kids during her adult life, but she did train dogs and knew a thing or two. She faced forward in her seat.

"I guess that means you don't want to play some of the nifty games made for kids on my tablet, then." She waited a full minute, then grinned when a syrupy-sweet voice piped up from the back seat.

"May I please play with your tablet?"

Chloe brought up a few proper games made for children and locked out the rest of the tablet.

She turned around and handed the device to Penny. "Here you go. See, that wasn't so bad."

She received a nose scrunch, but let it pass.

Ethan cleared his throat and looked in the rearview window. "Penny, I have to go out of town for a short period and you'll be staying with the babysitter until I return. She's a grown woman and I expect you to mind her."

Chloe glanced over her shoulder and snapped her head forward again. She didn't think Ethan had seen Penny's crestfallen expression a second before rebellion set in. The dejected look in the kid's face gripped Chloe's heart and refused to let go.

"I don't want to stay at the babysitter's. I want you to stay home," she screeched at an earsplitting decibel level.

Ethan's jaw locked. "I don't like your tone, young lady. This is related to work and you'll do as you're told."

Chloe slumped down in her seat. The hurt look she'd seen in Penny's eyes reminded her of the day she'd been told her parents were dead and that she'd be living at the orphanage. She had to do something, and then a thought occurred to her.

"Hey, Penny, if it's okay with your dad, why don't you stay at Mrs. Denton's? I'm sure the school bus could pick you up and drop you off there. That way you could have the run of the B and B and eat all the chocolate chip cookies you could ever dream of."

Chloe looked over her shoulder tentatively to see how her suggestion was received and was vastly relieved to see the calculating look on Penny's face. She'd take anything over the hurt.

The little stinker looked her straight in the eye and started bargaining. "Can Geordie stay with me?"

Chloe grinned. "It's always smart to stop while you're ahead, and my dog goes with me. I might need him."

"Can I, Daddy? Can I stay at Mrs. Denton's? I promise to be good."

Ethan looked at Chloe and mouthed *thank you*. It warmed her heart.

His grin belied the seriousness of his tone. "I don't know, Penny. Can I trust you to get on and off the bus at Mrs. Denton's and to mind what she says?"

Chloe laughed when Penny bounced in her seat, straining against the seat belt. "I promise, Daddy."

"If it's okay with Mrs. Denton, then you can stay there while I'm gone."

A happy squeal came from the back seat and Chloe smiled while Ethan parked the Jeep in front of the B and B. Her grin slid away when she thought about the disc and the man who was after her.

Mrs. Denton agreed readily to take care of Penny while he was away, and Ethan strode down the hall to tuck her in and say goodbye. Their flight left early the next morning and he would be long gone before Penny awakened.

He stopped at Penny's partially open door and was peeking through the opening when he heard whispers and several giggles from his daughter. What he saw surprised him. Chloe and Geordie were lying across the middle of the bed and Penny was sitting cross-legged near her pillow.

He strained to hear their words. "And this is how you keep Tommy Milton from putting frogs in your desk."

Chloe lowered her voice and Ethan grinned. He could only imagine what the woman was telling his daughter to do, but then they quieted.

"You know, Penny, nothing is going to happen to your father. He's a strong man and he's very good at what he does."

Penny's soft reply almost broke his heart. "But Chloe, Tommy Milton said Daddy could get killed in the line of duty and then I'd be all alone."

Ethan saw a big fat tear slide down her cheek, and his hands clenched. He had no idea that Penny worried something might happen to him.

He held his breath, ready to step in, while he waited on Chloe's response. She might not be the best person to be having this discussion with his daughter. The woman had lost both her parents at the same time, and she was a pretty tough lady.

Chloe didn't sugarcoat it. "Well, Penny, I can't promise you that nothing bad will ever happen, but you have to have faith in your dad. You're a powerfully strong reason for him not to get himself hurt because he loves you very much."

Penny perked up, and Ethan released the breath he'd been holding. "You mean like the preacher says to have faith in God?"

Chloe became evasive. "Something like that."

He watched Penny climb under the covers. "I'm going to say my prayers right now and ask God to take care of my daddy."

Chloe slid off the bed and Ethan slipped into a room across the hall. He didn't want Chloe to know he'd listened to their conversation. He was feeling a little raw at the moment, and he expected she was, too. He couldn't imagine a ten-year-old losing both parents at the same time, and he was sure Chloe's conversation with Penny had brought back sad memories.

Hearing Chloe's door close, he took a deep, fortifying breath. He thought he'd been doing a pretty good job raising Penny as a single parent, but discovering his little girl had been worrying that he would die had figuratively knocked the breath out of him. No six-year-old should have to worry about things like that.

He stepped into the hall and slipped into Penny's room. Moonlight filtered in through the window and he stared at the one thing he'd done right in his life. Pressing a soft kiss on Penny's brow, he stood for a moment longer and asked

God to look after his little girl. She opened her sleepy eyes and gifted him with a sweet smile before falling back asleep. One last look and he turned to leave. He had a few phone calls to make in preparation for his departure.

The next morning, Ethan was surprised to find Chloe at the kitchen table with her laptop and a mug of coffee sitting in front of her. Today she had on the same pair of jeans with a sweatshirt bearing another picture of her and Geordie competing in some kind of a bite contest.

"It's five o'clock. I figured you'd sleep until the last minute. We don't have to leave for the airport until six."

She grunted and took another sip of coffee without looking up.

"What's Geordie doing in the picture on your shirt?"

"Huh?" She looked up and he noticed dark blue circles under her eyes. "Oh," she said, rubbing her eyes, "I've trained Geordie in everything from tracking, to obedience and bite training. This was taken at an event we attended."

Ethan poured himself a cup of coffee and chuckled before taking a sip. "A trained attack poodle. I thought bite training was for dogs like German shepherds and Belgian Malinois. You know, dogs with a little muscle behind them."

Chloe's eyes narrowed until he grinned, letting her know he was teasing. He took a seat across from her and placed his mug on the table. "You've been up most of the night, haven't you?"

She rubbed her eyes again and dropped her hands in a defeated manner that roused his protective instincts. "I had to get my laptop set up so I could track my stolen computer."

"And?"

Her bleak eyes met his. "Ned was right. It's a good thing we already made flight plans because my old laptop is definitely in North Carolina."

He sensed there was much more. "And?"

Moisture filled her eyes, but she sat straight in her chair and took a deep breath. "If my tracking program is working right, my old laptop has been connected to the internet in Mocksville, North Carolina." She swallowed hard and whispered, "It's at the orphanage where I spent six years. Sarah Rutledge lives there. She took care of me during that time. She's the one who home-schooled me."

Ethan didn't like the way this was shaping up. "You think the killer is leading you to Sarah Rutledge? For what reason?"

Chloe exploded out of her chair and started pacing the floor. "I don't know!" she yelled, and faced him. "I don't know anything about a disc and I don't know how to stop this."

Ethan had been around Chloe long enough to know she was a woman who prided herself on her strength. Her tears proved she was beyond upset and it pinged him near the region of his heart, but he quickly discarded the emotion. He had no plans to get emotionally involved with this woman, or any woman—not after he'd failed Sherri. It was time for him to do his job.

"Sit down."

"What?"

A sparkle of fire lit her eyes, and he relaxed. He could deal with the fire much better than tears.

"Take a seat and let's make a plan."

She sat, and Ethan took another sip of coffee while thinking things through. "We'll follow the lead to North Carolina, and in the meantime, I think you should allow the killer to contact you."

A belligerent "Why?" sprang forth. "If he can't get in touch with me, I'll have more time to figure out what he wants."

Ethan raised a brow. "And what if he gets frustrated because he can't get in touch with you and decides to harm Sarah Rutledge?"

Chloe ran long, feminine fingers through her short tufted hair and blew out a breath. "Okay, okay, you're right. I can't take that chance." She leaned forward, her mouth a straight line. "Ethan, I don't have a clue what he wants."

"This is no different than solving a murder. We'll take it one step at a time. First we go to North Carolina and visit the orphanage. I don't know if the killer placing the laptop there is a threat to the people you know, or if there's something else he wants us to find, but that's our starting place. You with me?"

It was one of the few times she didn't try to hide her emotions.

"How can you be so calm?" Her tone was filled with annoyance and he almost grinned.

"I learned a long time ago to take things slow and methodical and to remove emotions from the equation."

Chloe looked like she wanted to deck him, and he finally did grin.

"I'm so glad you find this amusing."

The grin slid away and his jaw tightened. "I have two dead bodies on ice at the morgue. I don't find anything about this situation amusing. Grab Geordie and your bags and let's head to the airport."

She rose and Ethan watched her as she left the room. Chloe was full of ambiguity. One minute she was whipping out her gun, and the next she was easing a young girl's worries over her father possibly getting injured on the job. His stomach lurched when he thought about Penny's fears.

Fears he'd known nothing about that Chloe had discovered in a matter of days.

He was very confident in his ability to do his job, but he had failed both the women in his life. He should have realized how unhappy Sherri was, and he should have noticed Penny's worries.

There was a soft knock at the front door—he'd warned David not to ring the bell so Mrs. Denton and Penny wouldn't awaken—and he got up and stepped into the foyer. He glanced through the wavy glass built into the frame, then unlocked the door when he spotted David.

"Morning, Sheriff." David handed him a brown paper bag and gave him a speculative look. "You sure you want to do this?"

Ethan took the bag and ignored the question. "I'm not sure how long I'll be gone. Call me on my cell if anything happens at the station that you can't handle." He'd contacted his deputy early that morning with specific instructions.

"Yes, sir. 'Sides the two recent murders, not much happens around here." Disappointment filled David's voice and Ethan hid a smile as he nodded. His young deputy was eager for some action. He closed the door and slipped the paper sack inside his traveling bag, not sure he'd made the right decision. Only time would tell. Chloe Spencer had secrets, and he didn't know if some of them were connected to the two murders in his jurisdiction or the Peter Norris murder. All he knew for certain was that Miss Spencer was at the center stage of a murder investigation in New York, and somehow involved in the two murders in Jackson Hole. Just because she was nice to Penny was no reason to give her his trust. He'd treat this case like any other and gird himself against those cute dimples when they chose to appear.

ELEVEN

Finally they were seated on the plane and take-off was imminent. Geordie was allowed to sit with them because he could fit in a carrier under the seat in front of Chloe. She kept all his international shots and papers up-to-date because her job required her to travel when a company she had contracted with in the United States had offices in other countries. It didn't happen often, but she stayed prepared.

Ethan had been quiet on the way to the airport, and she wasn't in the best of moods herself. The plane finally lifted off and Chloe unbuckled her seat belt. She might as well get to work and open a pathway for the killer to get in touch with her. Ethan was right—if the killer couldn't get in touch with her, he might hurt someone else she knew.

Her fingers trembled slightly as she pulled her new laptop from the duffel she'd packed for the trip. Laying it across her lap, she opened the lid and turned it on. She stared at the screen while it booted up. What disc could she possibly have that someone was willing to kill for?

She was shaken from her morose thoughts when Ethan started talking.

"I'm not sure if I'm doing the right thing, but after what happened at Ned's, I decided to give you back your weapons. I went through proper TSA airport protocol and checked both our guns and the knife. You'll have them when we reach North Carolina."

Chloe felt a big ol' thump in the region of her heart. She was so happy she whipped her head up, grabbed Ethan around the neck and planted a big, fat kiss right on his lips. When she pulled back, he looked as stunned as she felt. Mortified to the soles of her boots, she started rambling.

"I didn't mean to do that. I'm so sorry. I was just so happy about getting my gun back—"

She snapped her mouth shut when she noticed the amusement on his face.

"It's not funny. I take it back."

He laughed. "You can't take back a kiss."

She felt heat crawl up her neck. "It didn't mean anything."

He sobered. "No, it didn't. Listen, Chloe, we're in the middle of an investigation—"

"And you don't trust me. I get it."

He looked like he wanted to say more, but shook his head.

She looked at him through the blurred tears and chuckled at his expression. His face held something close to a look of terror.

"I'm not crying because I don't cry." She swallowed past the lump in her throat. "I appreciate what you're doing. How did you manage that before we left?"

Relief flooded his face. "I called my deputy. He brought your gun and picked up a knife on the way to the house."

Chloe rubbed Geordie on his head when it popped up between her legs. She had partially unzipped the top of his collapsible dog crate. "So why are you handing back my weapons if you don't trust me?"

He seemed to give consideration to her question. She liked that about Ethan. He thought things through.

"If anything happens to me, I want you to be able to protect yourself."

Chloe nodded, but her heart expanded. Only a few people in her life had cared about her. She had often questioned her parents' love because the only thing they'd ever wanted was to save the world. Had they ever thought about what she'd endure if the worst happened and they were killed? Apparently not, because they'd died following their dream.

Chloe replayed the kiss in her mind. His lips were soft and sweet and felt good against hers, but she shook off the pretty thoughts. She wasn't a relationship kind of woman, and, besides, who would ever love her? She had a murky past, and even her parents hadn't loved her enough to give up the mission field. They had even quit taking her with them when she was four years old and she never knew why. They had always left her in the care of Sarah Rutledge at the orphanage when they left the country. They'd known the woman for years, so at least Chloe was familiar with Sarah and the orphanage when her parents' devastating deaths had occurred. Maybe they'd liked being alone, just the two of them, and a kid tagging along got in their way. Now she'd never know.

Burying the past, she got to work on her laptop. She probably had a zillion messages. She opened her email and proved herself right. She hated any kind of paperwork, and that included returning emails. She took a deep breath.

The first one on the list was from a dog client. She read several lines and laughed.

"Something funny?"

She positioned the laptop so he could see.

"What…is that dog doing?"

Chloe faced the computer and started talking and typing at the same time. "I told you I train dogs on the side. I only take a few clients at a time because most of my time is spent working in my security business. I don't have a kennel or anything. I go to the owners' houses and help with any kind of dog issues they're having. It's my passion and what I do for enjoyment. The dog in the picture is Byron. He's a full-size poodle and has fallen in love with the owner's riding lawn mower. He wants to eat beside it, sleep beside it, and pretty much spends all day lying beside it."

"Okay. So how do you fix that?"

"We're moving him away from it an inch at a time, hopefully getting him out of the garage and into the house. After he's able to sleep in the house at night, one morning he'll wake up and the lawn mower will disappear."

Ethan shook his head. "You're a multitalented woman, Chloe Spencer."

Chloe answered all her emails and pulled up the program tracking her old laptop. "My old computer is still at the orphanage. Should we warn Sarah before we arrive?" The thought of anything happening to the woman who had been so kind to her made Chloe sick to her stomach, and she lowered her head.

Two fingers lifted her chin, and she stared into a pair of sympathetic green eyes.

"Chloe, none of this is your fault. If everything is as you say, the fault lies with the killer." He pulled away and she missed the warmth of his callused fingers.

As the plane soared through the air, Chloe thought of returning to the orphanage and struggled quietly to breathe. She felt the past rising up to meet the present, and she didn't know if she was ready for that. She hadn't visited the orphanage since leaving at the age of sixteen. She'd kept in touch with Sarah by phone, but had tried her best to keep the past where it should be. Behind her, way behind her. Now the killer had given her no option.

Even though it was closed, her computer dinged, and Ethan's head turned sharply.

"What was that?"

She opened the lid. "Just an incoming email notification." She gasped out loud when she saw the notice.

Ethan leaned closer and touched her arm. "What is it?"

Chloe stared at the screen. "I opened the door for the killer, and it appears he took me up on the invitation. It's a live chat video feed." She looked up. "That means it's in real time and we'll be able to see and talk to each other. He's good. He found my new computer quickly after I opened my email."

Grim faced, Ethan nodded. "Turn the computer toward you and the window so he can't see me, then answer it."

She had lifted a finger to make it happen when Ethan grabbed her hand, stopping her. "Can you record it?"

She nodded, set the computer to Record, then opened the live chat.

The same masked face with evil eyes stared back at her from the computer screen.

"Miss Spencer, you've made yourself unavailable to me. That wasn't wise. I suggest you get to the orphanage as soon as possible. I understand you have a special friend there."

The screen went blank.

After watching the recording of the video, Ethan mulled over everything the killer had said. He'd detected a moment of uncertainty in the man's eyes, the only thing not covered by the ski mask.

"He's not sure you have the disc."

Her hand shook as she plowed fingers through her short hair and Ethan strangled his desire to take Chloe into his arms and reassure her. He was glad when she visibly pulled herself together.

"I don't have the disc, but what makes you say that?"

He shrugged. "In the course of my career, I've interviewed a lot of people. I learned to watch for signs that most people wouldn't notice. I saw uncertainty flash in his eyes."

Fire lit her eyes. "I'd give it to him if I had it. I want this to be over."

Ethan twisted in his seat and faced her. "Chloe, what if something dangerous is on that disc? Something that might hurt a lot of people?"

Her eyes flashed again, this time with hurt. "You think I have the disc." She swiped angry tears from her eyes. "You don't trust me."

She turned her face away and Ethan wanted to scream in frustration. He didn't know what to believe.

"Answer this question. Have you told me everything?"

She twisted back around, her face an emotionless mask. "I've told you everything pertinent to the investigation."

He gave it one last shot. "Chloe, I've learned that during the course of an investigation, a seemingly useless piece of information can crack a case wide open." She stayed quiet. "At least tell me this much—are your secrets connected to the case, or are they personal?"

"They're personal and none of your business."

"I'd suggest you give serious thought to sharing your past with me. It might be important."

She shook her head in denial. "He sent my old laptop there to let me know he can get to the people I love at any time."

Ethan sat back with a huff. Chloe was as stubborn as his daughter. The truth would ooze to the surface; it always did. One thing he did know—there were things in Chloe's past she didn't want revealed and he had to wonder why. Another thought crossed his mind. Chloe came up clean when David ran a search on her, but she was a computer genius. Could she have wiped a past criminal record clean? Ethan made a mental note to call in a few favors from people who owed him at his old department in Chicago. Chloe might be super skilled at computers, but there were still paper trails available. At least he hoped so.

"I think it's time to contact anyone you know in North Carolina who the killer might be interested in."

He knew he was being tough on Chloe, but reminding himself, as well as her, that she had a hoard of secrets kept his attraction to the woman in perspective. He wanted answers, but the investigation kept a much-needed wall between them. Not that he thought she was attracted to him. He had a ready-made family and Chloe was a strong-minded, independent businesswoman who owned her own security company and lived in New York.

Ethan eavesdropped unabashedly when the plane hit the ground and Chloe made a call on her smartphone. He grinned when she huddled next to the plane's window and lowered her voice.

"Sarah Rutledge, please. This is Chloe Spencer. It's an emergency. Yes, I'll hold."

She turned and glared at him. "Do you mind?"

He grinned. "Not at all."

She actually growled at him, and a second growl rose from under the seat. Geordie was following his handler's lead. She petted the dog's head through the dog carrier. Chloe presented him with the back of her head and cupped her hand over the side of the phone. He grinned wider. Hard to do with a smartphone. Technology was finally working in his favor.

"Sarah, hey, this is Chloe. I'm fine, and yes, I know it's been a while since I called. I miss you, too. Yeah, that's great. Congratulations. Listen, we can catch up soon. I'm on a plane headed your way. I should be there by late this evening. I'd appreciate that. Listen, there's something I need to tell you before I get there. I've run into a small problem." Chloe scrunched closer to the window. "No, not like last time, well, not exactly." Chloe took a deep breath and Ethan listened intently. "All you need to know right now is that you must be careful. Keep all the kids inside and lock the doors. Get the Taser I gave you and keep it on you at all times. Is it charged? Good. Get it now and I'll explain everything later. Thanks."

There was a long pause at Chloe's end of the conversation, and Ethan could only imagine what Sarah Rutledge was saying.

"Just do what I say, and everything will be fine. No! No need to call him. I'll be there soon. Yeah, I love you, too."

Chloe hit the end button and rested the hand holding her phone on her thigh.

"You gave Sarah Rutledge a Taser?"

She slipped the phone back inside her coat pocket. "It's a dangerous world. Everyone needs protection."

Ethan rested his head back and closed his eyes. He knew he appeared relaxed, but his mind was racing. "Who was the man you didn't want Sarah Rutledge to call?"

"It isn't pertinent to the investigation."

He heard the smirk in her voice, but let it go. "So what problem did you have last time?"

"What?" Frustration laced her words and that was fine with him because the woman frustrated him beyond words.

"You told Sarah you had run into a problem, then you responded 'No, not like last time, well, not exactly.'"

A finger poked him in the side and he opened his eyes. She had twisted fully around and was glaring at him. "Do you have one of those photographic memories where you can remember verbatim everything anyone says?"

Now she was aggravated and, well, welcome to his world. "No, I trained myself to listen and remember. You never—"

"I know, you never know when the smallest detail will crack a case wide open."

They both laughed, and it eased the tension until he asked, "So what was the problem you ran into last time?"

He was watching her closely and saw her left eye twitch. He'd hit a nerve.

"It's not pertinent to the investigation. It was a childhood prank, that's all."

He didn't believe her. She had failed to mask the emotion on her face, and tension and fear leaked past the carefully constructed facade. The closer they got to her past—North Carolina and the orphanage—the more her veneer crumbled.

They had rented a car and left the airport an hour ago. With Geordie watching intently from the cracked car door window behind her, Chloe now stood facing the front door of the sprawling orphanage's main office. She scanned the multiple unsecured buildings with unease. The killer could be anywhere.

She'd called Sarah five minutes ago and told her to be watching for them. The door opened and there she stood. The woman who had wrapped her arms around a lost ten-year-old girl whose parents had just been killed on the mission field. Maybe it was being at the orphanage for the first time since she'd left at age sixteen, but memories flooded her mind and Chloe almost staggered under the weight of it.

Once again, Sarah wrapped both arms around her and Chloe wanted to cry, but she refused to let her emotions have free rein. She was afraid that once released, the flood would begin and never stop. That didn't keep Sarah from crying her eyes out.

"Chloe, it's been too long, and I can't believe you're here. I know we've visited in New York, but I had given up hope that you'd ever come back here."

A throat clearing behind her had Chloe pulling out of Sarah's arms. "Sarah, this is Ethan Hoyt and he's here to help. That's Geordie watching us out the car window. Let's go inside."

The urgency in her voice must have prodded Sarah. Her red hair pulled back in a ponytail, she waved at Geordie and motioned them through the doorway. Once it was closed, she whirled around, her high energy almost visible to the eye. Sarah had always been bursting with life. She was the most positive person Chloe had ever met.

Sarah stuck a hand out toward Ethan. "It's always nice to meet a friend of Chloe's."

They shook hands and Ethan said, "Nice to meet you, too. Chloe has spoken highly of you."

Chloe rolled her eyes. The man could ooze charm when he wanted to.

Sarah grabbed a hand from each of them. "Come on. I know you're hungry. Let's get you something to eat, and after you've settled down, you can tell me what's going on." She pulled them toward the back door of the office building, chattering the whole way. As Chloe was intimately familiar with the place, she knew the kitchens were in the building right behind the office.

Sarah dropped their hands and moved several feet in front of them under the roofed open walkway connecting the buildings. Chloe checked out the other buildings and grounds visible from their location. Nothing had changed except that the place had deteriorated even more since she'd left. As she well knew, donations for the orphanage were hard to come by. She gave often, and the government helped, but the orphanage always ran on a shortage of funds.

Chloe looked forward and saw Sarah had almost reached the door to the kitchens, but suddenly, seconds after Geordie growled, Sarah was thrust backward and thrown to the old concrete walkway. Chloe froze. No! This couldn't be happening. She heard Ethan yelling, but it was as if the sound was being muffled by a loud roaring in her ears.

The paralysis left her body when Ethan ran forward and began ushering Sarah through the door. Chloe ran to the woman who had gotten her through the most traumatic part of her life and helped Ethan get her inside where it was safe.

Chloe knelt beside Sarah, whom they had gently laid on the floor, and she looked at Ethan, who was kneeling beside her. "Ethan," she whispered, not even realizing tears were streaming down her face, "help her."

Ethan ran his hands over Sarah in a brisk, professional manner, then rocked back on his heels. Though Chloe wanted to scream, she took a deep breath and collected herself.

"Ethan, is she okay?"

He shook his head, a quizzical expression on his face. "I'm not sure. The way she fell indicates she was shot, but she's breathing fine and there's no point of entry for a bullet wound. If there was a shot, the gunman used a silencer because I didn't hear anything."

Fury as she'd never known before tore through her body like a lightning strike. Chloe scrambled to her feet, and, without giving Ethan a chance to stop her, ran back outside, raised her arms in the air and screamed at the top of her lungs.

"You want a piece of me? Here I am. Take your best shot." She pumped a fist in the air. "But you even get close again to someone else I love, and you'll never get your hands on that disc. You hear me?"

A strong hand grabbed her by the arm and jerked her back onto the sidewalk and through the doorway.

She slapped Ethan's hands away and gulped in several deep breaths. It took a minute, but after calming herself, she ignored Ethan's dark scowl and dropped to her knees when Sarah moaned.

"Sarah, it's Chloe. Are you okay?"

Sarah opened her eyes and half smiled. "Things always were exciting when you were here, Chloe."

Tears filled her eyes, and Chloe leaned over and hugged the wonderful woman. Rising up, Chloe asked once again, "Are you okay?"

Sarah rubbed her chest and pulled out the large cross she wore at all times. It was attached to a long chain that reached her chest, close to her heart. She kissed the cross, held it up so she could take a look, then turned it around so they could see.

"God's hand at work."

Ethan kneeled across from Chloe and examined the cross. "Unbelievable."

"What? What is it?"

Ethan turned the cross so Chloe could see. The thick metal had a deep indentation about the size of a bullet in it. Chloe almost hyperventilated. So close. Sarah had come so close to dying, and it was her fault.

"Stop blaming yourself, Chloe, and help an older woman to her feet."

She and Ethan rose and each took an arm to pull Sarah up. As soon as she steadied herself, she cupped Chloe's face in her hands.

"Dear, sweet child, none of this is your fault. You always were one to take the weight of the world on your shoulders. I'm fine and, remember, only God knows when our time has come."

Chloe stepped back, immediately missing Sarah's warm touch. Frantically she looked around the familiar dining room that led to the kitchens in the back. The past she'd worked so hard to bury was a living, breathing thing bombarding her in waves.

A gentle hand took her by the elbow and led

her to one of the tables. "Come, sit down and let me get you something to eat."

Chloe numbly followed her orders and she heard Ethan talking low.

"Sarah, it's better if we don't call the police. We'll explain soon."

Sarah chuckled and mumbled something about keeping Chloe out of trouble, and Chloe's world righted itself. Her mentor was really okay. She had no doubt that Sarah would have a painful bruise where the bullet had hit the metal cross, but she always kept going no matter what, and that snapped Chloe out of her selfish trip to the past.

She jumped up from her seat, took Sarah by the arm and led her to a chair. "I'm sorry. I just zoned out for a moment. You're the one who needs to sit down. I'll grab us some grub and be right back."

On the way to the kitchen, her thoughts racing, Chloe desperately wondered which one of her loved ones the killer would target next.

TWELVE

Sarah released a huge sigh and smiled at Ethan. He took a chair across from her.

"You're sure you're okay? You don't need to see a doctor? Did you secure the kids like Chloe asked you to?"

She rubbed her chest again. "I'll be fine, and, yes, the kids and faculty are all safely indoors." Her smile melted away and Ethan got his first glimpse of the protective, mother hen side of Sarah. "But Chloe isn't okay. I want to know what's going on and how you're involved in it."

Ethan sat back and grinned.

"And what do you think is so funny about this situation, young man?"

"I see now where Chloe gets her feistiness. I know she's not your daughter, but from what she's told me about her past, she holds you in high regard. I believe she came to you at the age of ten and you were a large influence in her life." Ethan felt a little guilty for misleading the woman and making it sound like Chloe had shared her life story with him, but he needed information and he needed it fast. Things were escalating and the killer was becoming bold.

Her face softened. "It was longer than that. At about the age of four, Chloe's parents, who were my close friends, started leaving her with me when they were on the mission field. They didn't feel it was safe to take her with them because of some of the places they were assigned."

"Tell me about her parents."

Sarah abruptly sat up. "First you're going to tell me what's going on."

The woman was sharp, Ethan would give her that. His subtle interview tactic didn't work on her. Chloe stepped through a short set of swinging doors at the back of the room and approached the table with a large tray in her hands. Ethan's stomach growled and Chloe chuckled as she set the steaming dishes on the table in front of them. Ethan took the plate, silverware and napkin she handed him and waited until she was settled. Chloe nodded at Sarah and they bowed their heads. After a prayer was said, they began filling their plates.

Ethan moaned when he took the first bite of country-style steak. It melted in his mouth. Mashed potatoes followed, and he waved a fork in the air. "This is the best meal I've had in a long time."

Sarah nodded her head regally at the compliment, and Chloe started shoveling it in as fast as he did. Chloe finished first, daintily wiped her mouth with a napkin and looked at Sarah. "Did Ethan grill you while I was in the kitchen?"

Neither woman looked at him.

Sarah nodded. "I'm sure he did his best, but he could learn a thing or two from your adoptive father."

Ethan leaned forward, planting his elbows on the table. "You two ladies do know I'm sitting right here, don't you?"

They both laughed, and Ethan relaxed. He was itching to probe matters on exactly who Chloe's adoptive father was, but decided the best strategy would be to let them get comfortable. Maybe more information would slip out.

Sarah put on her teacher's face. "Now, I want to know what this is all about, and, Chloe—" she emphasized Chloe's name "—you better not leave anything out."

An unspoken message passed between the two women and Ethan filed it away to be examined later.

Chloe took a deep breath and told Sarah the same story she had shared with Ethan. The killer wanted a disc, but Chloe didn't know anything about it. She then explained who Ethan was, how they had met and why he had agreed to help her.

Ethan appreciated the sympathetic look Sarah graced him with before turning back to Chloe.

"You should call Stan."

Chloe firmed her lips and Sarah clammed up. *Who is Stan? This is the second time his name has been mentioned.*

"What can I do to help?" Sarah asked.

Ethan was amazed. There were no incriminations from Sarah, only love and support, even though she'd just been shot at. It also amazed him just how calm the two women were. It made him even more curious about Chloe's past.

Chloe leaned forward, placing her elbows on the table. "As I told you, I think the killer placed my laptop here so I'd know he could get to you at any time. We need to locate it to make sure it's nothing more than that."

Sarah turned her head and probed Ethan with her eyes. "And you, Sheriff Hoyt, why do you think the killer left Chloe's laptop here at the orphanage?"

He avoided looking at Chloe and kept his gaze on Sarah. "That's what we're trying to find out."

Sarah sat back in her chair and fingered the cross hanging around her neck. Everyone was quiet for several minutes, then Sarah rose to her feet.

"While you're here, there's something I need to give you." She gave Chloe an apologetic glance. "I wanted to wait for the right time, when I felt you were strong enough to handle it, and I believe that time is now."

Ethan stood and Chloe followed suit.

"What is it?" Chloe asked. There was a tremor in her voice, and Ethan wanted to comfort her, but kept his feet planted where they were. He held his breath. For some reason, he felt the next few minutes would rock Chloe's world, and there was nothing he could do to stop it.

"A letter," Sarah whispered back. "A letter your parents wanted me to give you if anything ever happened to them."

Chloe grabbed the back of a chair to steady herself. Ethan almost ran to her, but stopped himself. He had no idea what was going on. Even Sarah was keeping Chloe's secrets. He wanted to trust the woman, but it was evident that Sarah loved Chloe like a daughter, and he felt she'd do almost anything to protect her.

Chloe stepped away from Sarah, sadness and betrayal written on her face.

"Show me the letter."

Chloe almost strangled on the tidal wave of emotions threatening to drown her. Her parents had left her a letter and Sarah, a woman she'd loved since childhood, had kept it a secret. Her life was filled with secrets and the burden was growing wearisome.

Sarah reached out to touch Chloe's arm, but Chloe stepped back. She regretted the sad look in Sarah's eyes, but Chloe was barely holding it together. She forced her trembling hands to still when Sarah nodded.

"It's in the safe in my office."

Chloe followed Sarah, and Ethan fell in behind them. He took the lead at the door and hurried them through the open walkway. When Chloe stepped into the familiar office, the warmth of the past surrounded her. There was a small, battered table sitting in front of the only window. It was where Chloe had done her studies while Sarah took care of the orphanage's massive amount of paperwork.

Ethan took a seat in one of the two chairs placed in front of Sarah's ancient desk. He slid Chloe a glance when she sat in the one beside him.

"You okay?"

His voice sounded gruff and she almost smiled. Men generally didn't handle emotional women very well. For some reason, his concern balanced her. She drew in a deep breath. She could do this. She had survived far worse and she needed to push the emotion aside. She'd handled mean, aggressive dogs and helped them conform to society's expectations. She could handle this emotional roller coaster. She grinned. Ethan reminded her of some of her dog cases. He'd been wounded, and maybe as payback for helping her, she might be able to help heal the deep wound he was carrying around from losing his wife.

Sarah slowly stood from her crouched position in front of the small safe hidden behind a panel built into the wall. Chloe scooted out of her chair and took Sarah by the elbow. She felt like scum when Sarah sent her a grateful look. Full of guilt and love, Chloe threw her arms around her mentor and friend.

"I'm sorry. I'm acting like a jerk. I know you were only following my parents' instructions."

There were tears in Sarah's eyes when they pulled apart, and Sarah touched Chloe's cheek. "You always were my favorite. God has great plans in store for you."

Chloe didn't respond but smiled instead and retook her seat. She didn't know what God had in store for her, but she couldn't trust that He would take care of this situation. She would handle that job herself. God had let her down one time. She wouldn't lose anyone else she loved.

Chloe watched, her heart in her throat, as Sarah unbuckled an old leather satchel and pulled out a standard-sized envelope. Reaching forward slowly, Chloe took the envelope and stared at her name written on the front. Her parents had held this envelope in their hands. Shaking off the nostalgia, she carefully tore the glued flap open, pulled out a sheet of paper and started reading.

My dear, sweet Chloe, if you are reading this letter, you're a grown woman now and we're no longer with you because God had other plans. Please know that we love you deeply, which is why we left you at the orphanage with Sarah when we were in the mission field and things became dangerous. I was torn between your care and the Lord's calling. I did my best to fulfill my duty as a mother and my duty as a child of God.

The reason I'm writing this letter now is because your father and I suspect that we have been betrayed and our lives are in danger. If in the future you find yourself in any sort of unexplainable trouble or danger, please tell Sarah to contact Stan. He knows everything that's going on. Darling, if the danger is related to what we're involved in, please know that the answers lie in the past.

Do you remember your special place where you always loved to hide things? I remember one time you hid your father's car keys there and he had to bribe you with a trip to the zoo before you would tell us about your secret place.

Please know that your father and I love you dearly, and God is always with you.
Your loving mother,
Adelia

Her trust shattered into a million pieces, but Chloe only felt emptiness and a deep gaping void inside. She lifted her head and stared at the woman she had trusted with such absoluteness.

"You knew who Stan was before…" Chloe clamped her lips shut when she became acutely aware of Ethan listening.

A big tear rolled down Sarah's face and she said beseechingly, "I'm sorry. Yes, I knew Stan—" she glanced at Ethan and then back at Chloe "—before."

Ethan gently took the letter from her hand and she released it.

He read the letter, then lifted his head and looked at Sarah. "You knew Stan before what?"

Chloe grabbed the letter from his hand and handed it to Sarah so she could read it.

"That's not pertinent to the case." Chloe didn't want Ethan to know about Stan because she knew he would go digging and her past would be revealed.

A low growl emanated from Ethan and she wanted to laugh. Her sorrow lifted when she gazed into his disgruntled face. She watched Sarah finish reading the letter, and the older woman slowly shook her head in the negative. So she didn't know anything about the danger her parents were speaking of.

Chloe stood. "I need to check on Geordie soon so we should go ahead and search for my old laptop. According to my tracking program, it's here on the orphanage grounds. Let's go find it." She would assess the letter and its hidden meanings later, in private.

THIRTEEN

Ethan's mind was processing and sorting information at a rapid rate. He wanted to know who Stan was and how he was connected to Chloe, and he wanted some answers about the letter, but those questions would have to wait. Chloe was right. They needed to find the laptop, and he had to make sure Sarah and the orphanage stayed safe until they caught the killer.

"My laptop gave us this general vicinity, but it won't pinpoint the exact location," Chloe said, interrupting his thoughts. She looked at Sarah. "Does the orphanage still have an internet connection?"

Sarah nodded. "It's the same as it used to be. We have two phone lines for computer use. One here in my office, and one available to the students. Since mine is connected to my own computer, I suggest we check the one in our small library."

Ethan followed the two women through a

maze of halls, his thoughts on Chloe. With each new piece of information that came forth, he was beginning to realize Chloe Spencer wasn't as prickly and tough as she liked people to believe. Oh, she was tough, but when she had spoken to Penny about the school bully, she sounded soft and tender in her own way.

Ethan also considered what he knew about her background so far. She had a tendency to run when things got dicey. Chloe was literally a computer genius. She trained dogs, which correlated with the soft heart thing. Losing her parents at the tender age of ten and growing up in an orphanage must have affected her tremendously. She owned a successful security company. He admired the tenacity it took for her to overcome her past and become a successful woman.

He couldn't imagine the things she'd gone through. His wife had died unexpectedly and his mom had passed away, but he was beginning to realize his problems were simple compared to those of the woman walking in front of him.

He still had his dad, Penny, and his sister, Carolyn, and her family. How many people did Chloe have in her life? People who cared about her. He made a mental note to inquire after they found the laptop.

Sarah veered into a small, tidy room filled with books and study tables. A couple of young residents had their noses stuck in books, but they looked up when their little group entered. Sarah moved to the corner of the room and peered under a table, looking for the phone line. When she stood up, her face was ashen and she held a laptop in her hand.

"Is this what you're looking for?"

Ethan knew why she was upset. The killer, or one of his flunkies, had gotten very close to the children in the orphanage in order to place Chloe's laptop in the library. He could have harmed any one of them, and Ethan suspected that was one of the points of the exercise.

He reached out to take the computer, but Chloe stepped in front of him.

"Let me. If he's online, waiting for me to open it, I don't want him to see anyone but me."

Ethan nodded. "Okay, but record it if he's on there."

Ethan was very good at picking up things no one else noticed. Mannerisms, facial movements or tics, among other things.

"I will." Chloe took a deep breath and sat down with the computer facing the wall.

Sarah gave Ethan an appreciative nod when he helped her to a chair. They both watched as Chloe slowly opened the laptop. Her mouth tightened, and Ethan knew the killer was waiting for her on a video chat.

"Miss Spencer, I see you found my little gift."

Ethan was impressed when Chloe's mouth curled at the corners in a false smile. "I did." She leaned forward. "And if you even think of approaching or shooting at one of my friends again, I'll make sure you never get that disc, even if I have to die to make that happen."

Ethan's stomach roiled when he saw the truth in Chloe's eyes. She would do what she said. He wanted to applaud her for standing up to the killer, but he didn't like that she so easily placed herself in danger. The killer could react in several ways, based on how badly he wanted the item. Ethan held his breath, waiting for a response.

The killer barked out a manic laugh and his voice turned sly. "Miss Spencer, you remind me of your mother with all that black hair and pixie face."

As the color drained from Chloe's cheeks, Ethan stood, ready to call a halt to the proceedings, but she waved a hand for him to back off. Against his better judgment, he sat down.

Chloe's hands were clenching the sides of the laptop, but her expression was a blank slate.

"How do you know my mother, and why did you bring her up?"

"Haven't you ever wondered why your parents started leaving you behind with Sarah when they were on the mission field?" The killer taunted her instead of giving a direct answer. "Most missionaries take their children with them. Maybe they didn't love you." Ethan had to restrain himself from marching around the desk and blasting the killer himself.

Ethan was bursting to explode into action. It was painful to watch Chloe maintain a facade of indifference when Ethan knew this was shredding her heart.

With no inflection in her tone, Chloe said, "The past has no bearing on this. Tell me about the disc, and I'll try and find it. Why do you think it's in my possession?"

There was a short pause. "So you don't know about it? I was afraid of that. I know you're recording this, and I also know about that small-town sheriff traveling with you, so I can't tell you much. Examine your parents' past and you'll find what I want." There was another pause. "I'll leave your friends alone for the time being, but if you don't make your technology available for me to stay in touch, I'll kill them first, then I'll come after you."

Chloe sat back in her chair, staring blankly at the computer. Ethan assumed the killer had signed off, or whatever. Just as he was about to say something, Chloe lifted her head and stared at Sarah. "I need to know everything."

Ethan's heart was bleeding for Chloe because, for the first time since he'd met her, across her face flitted a myriad of conflicting emotions, evident for anyone to see.

Sarah was wringing her hands. She looked heavenward, mumbled a few words, then looked back at Chloe.

"Let me tell you everything I know. I'll start at the beginning."

Chloe's face went stony, and Ethan was afraid that whatever Sarah had to say would affect her deeply. He was beginning to care for the woman, and he didn't like what was happening to her. He could almost see the walls being constructed around her heart.

"Please do."

She was so formal with the woman who had helped raise her. Ethan was right, Chloe was preparing herself for heartache.

Sarah took a deep, shaky breath. "I don't know a lot, but first, let me assure you that your parents loved you very much. When you were around four years old, they told me their mission assignments were in dangerous places and asked that I take care of you while they were away. Shortly before they died, they were home on furlough and gave me that letter to give to you should something happen to them." She paused. "I sensed something was wrong, but your mother just laughed and assured me I was borrowing trouble. That feeling of doom never left me." Tears were rolling down both of Sarah's cheeks. "Several weeks after they went back into the field, I was notified that they'd been killed by one of the local gangs in the area. The criminals were never caught."

With methodical movements, Chloe stood and slowly closed the lid to the laptop. She lifted her head and, in an almost conversational tone, said, "I'm going to find the person, or people, responsible for murdering Peter Norris and my parents."

Automatically Chloe compartmentalized the tidal wave of emotions bearing down on her when Ethan said, "We should get going, and you need to check on Geordie."

Briskly she unplugged her old laptop and tucked it under her arm. She didn't want to look up because she was torn. Sarah had practically been a mother to her during the most horrific time of her life, but Chloe was battling a feeling of betrayal. That all changed when she lifted her head. Sarah stood there, hands folded primly in front of her, her expression reminding Chloe of a shattered picture frame.

Chloe's heart constricted. She couldn't leave things this way. What if she failed in her mission to retrieve the disc and Sarah ended up dead because of her? She moved around the desk, shoved the laptop into Ethan's arms and wrapped her own arms around Sarah. Sarah started rubbing her back, much like she had done when Chloe was a lost four-year-old. Warmth and love permeated her body.

Chloe pulled back. "I don't think I've ever properly thanked you for all you did for me."

Tears streaming down her face, Sarah touched Chloe's cheek. "Haven't you figured it out? You're the daughter I never had."

Chloe gave her another quick hug and headed out of the office before she fell apart. For years she'd dodged a multitude of emotional bullets, but the past was catching up with her. She heard Ethan mutter a quick goodbye, then he reached her and charged in front before she could open the front door.

"Let me go first."

"He won't kill me until I find the disc. Before then, I think we're safe. After that, all bets are off." She knew she sounded confident and sure of herself and the situation—a persona she'd perfected over the years—but the truth was far different. A mixture of anger, helplessness and betrayal churned in her gut, emotions she'd never allow the world—or Ethan—to see.

There were no further incidents on the way to

their vehicle. After reaching the car and getting Geordie out for a short bathroom break, they all loaded up and Chloe stared at the orphanage.

"I know what I said earlier, but do you think Sarah is safe?"

"We could still call the police, get the incident on record."

She snorted. "Yeah, and they'll send a car by to cruise the grounds a couple times a day. This guy is smart. If he wants to take someone out, the local police aren't going to be much help."

"I think we're dealing with a highly trained individual."

Chloe whipped her head around. "You think he's police or military?"

Ethan started the engine. "Maybe. Peter Norris's death was planned with precision. Our killer has experience."

They sat there with the car idling, and Chloe became curious about the man sitting next to her.

"I know about Penny, and I know what you and Mrs. Denton told me about your wife—"

"Sherri, her name was Sherri."

"Okay, Sherri, but what about the rest of your life? Do you have any siblings? Are your parents alive?"

At first, she didn't think he was going to answer, but then he shrugged his shoulders. "My life hasn't been as eventful as yours. My dad has a small ranch in Jackson Hole—that's where I grew up. I have an older sister. Her name is Carolyn, and she and her husband, Bill, have two daughters, Sylvia and Tracy, both under the age of five."

"And your mom?"

He stared out the driver's window, and Chloe figured there was more to the story than he was telling.

"She died when I was in college." He turned back to her. "Why all the questions?"

She had to ask herself the same thing, and if she was completely honest, she'd have to admit that she liked Sheriff Ethan Hoyt. He was the most straight-up guy she'd ever met, and he was a big, mushy teddy bear when it came to dealing with his daughter. She often wondered how her life would have turned out if at least one of her parents had lived.

But it didn't matter whether she liked him or not, because her past was catching up with her fast, and if he ever found out what she'd done when she was sixteen, well, she could only imagine the disgust on his face. She didn't want to deal with that, so she fell back on her flippant attitude and shrugged.

"Just curious. I figure if my past is going to be belched up, we should even the playing field."

"Lovely choice of words, Miss Spencer. We

need to plan our next move. Let's take another look at the letter your mother left you."

And that statement put things back on an even keel.

Chloe pulled the letter from her pocket. "Looks like we're going to dredge up more of my past." She reread the letter, careful to keep the emotion attached to it at bay. "My mom and dad suspected a betrayal and that their lives were in danger. And I'm definitely in an unexplainable and dangerous situation, that's for sure. She told me to contact Stan and that the answers lie in the past. Then she tells the story about when I hid Dad's car keys in my secret place."

Chloe looked at Ethan. "Do you think it's possible they had a disc of some kind and hid it in my secret place?" Adrenaline shot through her body. This was the first real clue they had, and she hoped it would lead them to the truth even though her parents having a disc the killer wanted raised even more questions, like why didn't they call Stan themselves? Was it to protect her?

"I think it's a high probability."

Chloe got the feeling that Ethan was putting things back on a professional footing after their emotional bonding. That was fine by her. He would never be interested in someone like her anyway, though she had to admit it did hurt a little. Pushing aside any remote dreams of happily-ever-after, Chloe settled more comfortably in her seat and thought about the letter.

"What I'd really like to know is what my parents were involved in."

Were her parents really even missionaries, or were they…something else entirely?

FOURTEEN

As Ethan drove the car toward the house where Chloe had grown up, he thought about everything that had happened at the orphanage. It had been an emotionally charged meeting. He glanced at her and then back at the road, but she didn't look upset. He'd been around her long enough to know she was a master at hiding her feelings.

His hands tightened on the steering wheel. He didn't want to be attracted to her. He was trying hard to keep things professional between them so nothing would come of it, but seeing her with Sarah shed a whole new light on Chloe Spencer. She might carry enough weapons on her person to handle any situation, but her spiked short black hair, Harley and leather clothes hid something buried deep. Something soft and loving. Something he wasn't sure he wanted to delve into. He reminded himself he still didn't have all the facts. She was hiding something, and that should be enough to keep his thoughts on the case.

"Don't worry, you're off the hook."

Her words caught him off guard. "What?"

She shrugged and turned her head away from him, staring out the passenger window.

"You're a small-town sheriff. I live in New York. You live in a black-and-white world, and me—" she turned and flashed him a sad smile "—not so much."

The whole conversation made him uncomfortable. "I don't know what you're talking about." Although he did, and, obtusely, he didn't like her telling him how he should feel, even though he agreed with her. Still, that sad smile clenched his gut and wouldn't let go.

Against his better judgment, he said, "You want to talk about it?"

She snorted out a laugh. "That came across sounding like you'd rather walk on a bed of nails."

They both laughed, and Ethan turned down the quiet street Chloe indicated.

"It's the fourth house on the right."

There were cars parked in the driveway. Ethan passed by the house, turned around and pulled the car to the curb across the street. He cut the engine and stared at the place where Chloe had grown up. It was in an old North Carolina neighborhood and the house was brick, a typical ranch style. It had a double garage, a small front porch and a cement walkway with a few weeds struggling to survive growing through the cracks.

Neither of them said anything for a few moments.

"My life hasn't been perfect, you know."

Chloe didn't respond, but tilted her head, watching him like a curious dog.

"Forget it," he said, and reached for the door handle.

A small, delicate hand touched his and he froze. He didn't so much as move a muscle. It was amazing how much warmth radiated from such a petite hand.

"Ethan, maybe you haven't been through the same things I have, but they're no less traumatic. Losing your mother, then your wife, and you've done an amazing job with Penny."

He looked at her hand on top of his. He couldn't do this. He wasn't ready. And even if he was, Chloe wasn't exactly a home-and-hearth kind of girl.

As her hand slowly slid away, he felt as if he was losing something important, something vital to his life, but he allowed it to happen.

She got out of the car, tapped the roof and leaned in through the open car door. Gone was the warmth, and in its place was the old Chloe, the one he'd first met. The feisty fireball, ready to take on the world, but now he knew differently. He'd gotten a glimpse of the real Chloe and he mourned the loss.

"Are you coming, or not? I know a way we can sneak in through the backyard. My secret hiding place is back there. The owners will never know we're there."

Ethan shook his head. This was exactly why nothing would ever work between them.

He got out of the car and started walking toward the front of the house. He heard Chloe slam her car door shut. She grabbed his arm when she caught up with him.

"What are you doing?"

He lifted a brow. "I'm going to the front door to show my credentials, explain the situation and ask permission to be on their property."

He almost laughed when she rolled her eyes, reminding him of Penny.

"And what if they call the cops, Mr. Go by the Rules?"

He grinned, glad to be concentrating on Chloe's taciturn nature rather than her inquisitive brown eyes. "You don't have to say anything. I'll tell them there's an ongoing investigation and their cooperation would be greatly appreciated."

She rolled her eyes again. "You really are

naive, you know that? People don't just cooperate. If it were me, I'd demand a warrant."

Ethan moved forward. "I've found that most people aren't as mistrustful as you and are willing to help."

"Yeah, we'll see about that, Mr. Squeaky Clean."

Chloe grunted as she pushed the shovel into the ground with her foot. Not only had the owners agreed to allow them onto the property, they had provided a shovel when she admitted to Ethan her secret hiding place was an old metal box buried in the ground beside the gazebo.

A gauntlet of emotions had almost crippled her when she stepped into the backyard. The swing attached to the huge oak tree was gone, but the gazebo her father had built one summer was still standing. It needed a paint job, but the bones of it had weathered well against time.

"I told you I'd do that."

Chloe ignored Ethan. She told him she'd do the digging because he got them onto the property, but the truth was that she needed to do something physical to ward off the memories attached to the place.

Her shovel hit metal and she fell to her knees, swiping away the dirt. The top had a handle and she cleared enough dirt to pull it out of the ground. Placing it in front of her, she reached for the latch but jerked her hand back when it trembled. All of a sudden, she didn't want to know what was in the box. Had her parents been involved in something illegal? Were they even real missionaries?

Two strong hands reached down and raised the box off the ground. "Let me open it."

Chloe didn't argue, but she did look up when Ethan chuckled and lifted something out of the box.

"Is this what I think it is? I wouldn't have taken you for that type of girl."

Chloe scrambled to her feet and gently took the fragile old doll from his hand. She choked back a sob, stared at the doll and fingered it softly. "This was the last thing my mother bought me before they were killed." She choked out a laugh. "All the girls my age wanted Barbie dolls, but I wanted this one because she was less known and more unique."

Before she could get too emotional, Ethan pulled out something else and held it up, something she was very familiar with.

"This is the only other thing in here."

Chloe took the disc from his hand and grinned. "Bingo!" Her euphoria didn't last for long. If there was something on there that implicated her parents, she wanted to be rid of it as soon as possible. She slipped it into her jeans pocket.

"Let's go to the car. I'll contact the killer and get this over with."

His hand gripped her arm when she tried to slip past. "Not so fast. Chloe, you know we can't just give this to the killer. We need to follow through and find the truth." He paused. "Even if it hurts."

Chloe jerked her arm from his grip and walked a few steps away. He was right, she knew that. She just didn't know if she could deal with finding out her parents had lied to her. Chloe hadn't trusted God in a long time, but if she found out her parents had betrayed Him, where would that leave her?

She shook off his hand. "Fine. Let's get in the car and I'll open it on my laptop. We can discuss it after we see what's on there."

Ethan picked up the shovel and repaired the hole they'd dug, then propped the shovel against the gazebo.

He took her by the arm and led her toward the car while scanning both ends of the street. His actions made Chloe shiver.

"You think he's watching us now?"

His jaw was locked and his mouth grim. "I don't know if he's working alone or has hired guns, but he's been one step ahead of us the whole time."

Ethan tugged her forward. "If you're going to

blow your top at the thought, please wait and do it in the car where it'll be safer."

His exasperated tone quickly defused her anger. She almost smiled and did as he asked. As soon as they were in the car and headed down the road, Chloe opened her laptop and waited for it boot up, then inserted the disc. She leaned back and waited, processing everything that had happened.

"Ethan, do you think the killer had something to do with my parents' deaths?" Now that she'd gotten past the emotional turmoil of revisiting her past at the orphanage and her old home, she was thinking more clearly.

She twisted around in her seat so that she was facing him. "Think about it. He led me back to the orphanage and told me to examine my parents' past." She faced forward again and, for the first time since her parents had died, mentally walked through her past, something she'd never done before. Something she had deftly avoided. With startling clarity, Chloe realized she'd been on the run her whole life and had never come to terms with her past. Was that why she'd never dated guys more than two or three times—because she could never stay still long enough to form a relationship?

Slowly she said, "Ethan, why now? Why is

the killer coming after the disc now? If it's connected to my parents' deaths, why not sooner?"

Ethan tapped a finger on the steering wheel. Chloe was beginning to learn his mannerisms, which was probably not a good idea, considering their attraction could never go anywhere.

"Didn't you say Sarah homeschooled you, even though the other kids attended a regular school? You were pretty much off-the-grid. Did you change your last name when you were adopted?"

And the lightbulb was lit. "He couldn't find me," she said, still speaking slowly. Her computer dinged an alert and Chloe was snapped out of her musings.

"No, no, no, no, no!" Chloe's fingers flew over the keyboard. "Stupid, stupid, stupid. I should have gone offline."

Ethan kept quiet and she appreciated that. She explained what was happening while she tried to shut the program down as fast as she could. "I'm so stupid! I knew he had access to this computer. Why did I insert the disc? He's trying to steal the information."

Chloe typed as fast as she could, but lifted her fingers when a new person entered the equation. "What's this?"

"What's what?" Ethan asked as he slowed the car and pulled off to the side of the road.

It took Chloe a moment to recognize the intruder, but she grinned when she did.

"The cavalry has arrived and he's helping me stop the killer from stealing the information on the disc."

"Who's the cavalry?" Ethan's tone was cool and controlled. Another thing Chloe liked about him. He was calm under fire.

"I do believe it's our mountain man."

Ethan snorted and eased the car back onto the road.

Chloe hit a final key and, with help from Ethan's friend, stopped the killer from accessing the information. She glanced up at Ethan with the fire of cyber battle in her eyes.

"We won. The killer only got a sliver of what's on the disc."

"Could you tell what was on it?"

Chloe shook her head. "No, it looks like it's in code." And she knew what that meant. A trip to New York and another blast from the past.

That meant trying to figure out a way to tell Ethan about Stan while keeping her past a secret and staying away from the police.

"Hold on!" Ethan yelled, and Chloe stiffened.

Geordie started barking in the back seat, and she braced herself. They were on a curvy back road and she glanced in the rearview mirror. A nondescript four-door car was fast approaching their rear. All of a sudden, her computer dinged a message. She glanced at Ethan. His jaw was taut and his eyes were glued to the road.

"Answer it," he ground out. "It might be the killer. I'm sure he followed us to your old home and now he knows we have the disc."

Chloe wanted to kick herself. If she hadn't been so impatient to see what was on the disc, she wouldn't have made a beginner's mistake.

Releasing her grip on her armrest, she opened her laptop. "You're right. It's a message from the killer. I don't know if he's in the car behind us or sitting in an office several states away and one of his hirelings is following us, but he says to stop and give the disc to the driver or we both die, along with my friends." Her voice wobbled at the end of the sentence, and that just made her fume.

Ethan drove fast but steadily for a minute or so. "Do you have another backup disc?"

"A decoy?"

"Yes. Do you have one?"

Chloe wanted to kick herself. "No." Right after she spoke, her computer dinged again. She looked down and grinned. "But I don't think it matters. Listen to this. 'You owe me one.' It's signed RBTL."

Ethan grinned. "Read Between the Lines."

"Yep, I do believe it's your mountain man at

work." Chloe transferred the information on the disc to her computer, then hit a few keys.

Ethan glanced at her. "What are you doing?"

Chloe mimicked a Southern lady. "Why, Ethan, I'm wiping the disc clean," she said as she slipped it into a protective cover, "then you're going to throw it out the window where our company can see it real clearly."

His grin widened. "Let's do it."

Her computer chirped. She pulled the disc out and handed it to Ethan. He waited until they were on a straight stretch of road, but Chloe stopped him. "Wait! Let me send a message to the killer."

She typed quickly and grinned at Ethan. "Now!"

He threw it out the driver's window and the car behind them hit the brakes and swerved in the road. Ethan looked at her and grinned. "Good job."

His praise warmed her in a place that had been cold for a long time, until she remembered they didn't have any kind of a future, even if they both were interested in one. Chloe shook off the thought and knew what she had to do.

"I pray that Sarah stays safe, and we have to go to New York." She took a deep breath. "I need to tell you about Stan…"

FIFTEEN

Ethan was impressed by the woman sitting in the car next to him. Not many people he knew would have been so calm under fire. She was tough as nails on the outside, but what drew him was the softer side she kept safely tucked away. But the woman still had secrets, and he had a strong feeling one of them was about to be revealed. He had long wondered about the mysterious Stan. In one way, he didn't want to know. Was Stan a boyfriend? An ex-boyfriend? No, that wouldn't fit the timeline if her parents knew him all those years ago. The man would be old enough to be her father.

He pushed aside his—*jealousy?*—and girded himself for another truth to be revealed. "You were saying?" he prodded after her sentence trailed off.

She cleared her throat and he figured this must be hard for her.

"Stan is my adoptive father."

"I assume he lives in New York and we're headed to the airport?"

She chuckled roundly. "You're quick on the draw. Yes, Stan and Betty live in New York." She took a deep breath and turned away, staring at the passing scenery. "They adopted me when I was sixteen. They were never able to have children."

Something didn't add up. "Most people adopt babies. How did they find you at an orphanage in North Carolina?"

She shrugged evasively and Ethan's lie detector was activated.

He thought about everything she'd gone through and shuddered when he thought about his own daughter. He couldn't imagine Penny living through what Chloe had gone through.

"Were you happy?"

She looked at him and her dimples popped out when she grinned. "Even though I was sixteen, I was a terror, but they loved me anyway. Eventually, I turned into a good upstanding citizen."

It was a quiet ride the rest of the way to the airport. Flights were expensive, but they got tickets on the next plane to New York. They checked their weapons, and soon Geordie was tucked in a crate under the window seat in front of Chloe. Ethan took the aisle seat. Once they were airborne, Chloe laid her head back and closed her eyes.

Ethan studied her. It was the first time he'd been able to do so without being obvious. Her spiked black hair somehow worked for her. It showcased her pixie face and highlighted her brown eyes. The dimples had disappeared for the moment, but they always grabbed his gut when she smiled.

"You're fortunate to have Penny, and even though you've managed to spoil her rotten, she's a good kid."

Ethan thought about his daughter, and he hated to admit it, but Chloe was right. He blew out a breath. "I tried too hard to make up for her mother's death. She was so young when Sherri died, but you're right. I need to set more boundaries."

Her eyes were still closed, and he wondered where this was leading.

"Were you happy in your marriage? I know you said Sherri didn't quite fit in after the move to Jackson Hole."

"Happy enough, I suppose."

He looked away, not wanting Chloe to see the sense of failure in his eyes. He turned back around when a soft hand found his and squeezed. "Ethan, you did what you thought was right. Sherri should have told you if she was unhappy."

Sadness engulfed him. "Maybe, but she was gone so quickly."

Chloe held on to his hand. "You never got closure. I understand that."

He felt like a heel. Of course Chloe understood. She never got to say goodbye to her parents. At least he was with Sherri right before she died.

"I'm sorry about your parents."

She shrugged, but he now knew there was emotion churning beneath the careless gesture.

"So what about you? Have you ever been in a serious relationship?"

She flashed humorous brown eyes at him. "Well, since we're having our own private therapy session, I've had an epiphany of my own. I've dated, but never the same guy more than two or three times. I've recently realized I've spent my adult life running from my past, but I'm ready to stand and fight now."

He grinned. "Somehow that doesn't surprise me. And speaking of fighting, don't you think it's time for you to tell me more about Stan and why you think he can help us?" This wasn't only about the case. He wanted to know all of Chloe's secrets.

He was right. It was time for Chloe to fess up, but she'd never, ever tell him about her juvenile record. All this time, she'd been afraid that telling him about Stan would unveil her past, but she'd be careful not to reveal too much. She really liked Ethan, and never wanted to see the inevitable look of disappointment if he found out the truth.

"As I said, Stan and Betty are my adoptive parents. They couldn't have any kids of their own. It was a good fit because I love technology and Stan is Director of the Criminal, Cyber, Response and Services Branch of the FBI."

His head snapped around and astonishment filled his face.

"What? Are you telling me that your adoptive father is a director in the FBI and you didn't go straight to him right after you witnessed the murder? Why?"

His tone was demanding and accusatory, and she didn't like it.

"Not that I have to tell you anything, but I didn't want to bring danger to his doorstep."

Ethan closed his eyes and took a deep breath, as if he was trying to fortify himself. He blinked his lids open and stared at her. "Chloe, I would lay down my life for my daughter. Don't you think your adoptive father would do the same? I imagine he and your adoptive mother have worried themselves sick over you."

Chloe flashed him an annoyed look.

"What?"

She sniffed. "I don't like it when you're right."

Ethan barked out a laugh. "You'll keep whoever you marry on his toes, that's for sure."

The look of consternation that crossed Ethan's face would have made her laugh if his statement hadn't made her so sad. He had all but said that man wouldn't be him. She turned away. It wasn't as if he'd made any overtures in that department, and even if he had, she couldn't really reciprocate.

Chloe shook it off. They had work to do and a killer to catch.

"Chloe, I'm sorry. I didn't mean to insinuate that there was the possibility of a relationship between us."

She slipped on an invisible mask and looked at him. "It's nothing. You asked me how Stan could help us. As I told you, he's head of the cyber department. He has access to programs the average citizen doesn't know about." She should know—she'd used those programs while tracking down a handful of criminals for the FBI while she was working off her community service.

"They also have people who specialize in decoding. That disc was made so many years ago, we might have a hard time deciphering the information."

"What about Stan and the FBI? I thought you wanted to stay away from law enforcement."

She had prepared for that. "We'll start without them. I have a plan."

He rolled his eyes. "Of course you do, and what, may I ask, is your brilliant idea? And it better be legal."

Chloe grinned. She could deal with this. It was much better than thinking about their non-relationship. "Before we resort to using Stan's resources to find the killer, I'm going to try finding out what's on the disc myself. That would give me leverage in case someone turns me in, since police questioning would take away precious time I need to catch this guy before someone else gets hurt. Though I beefed up the security on my computer, it's only a matter of time before the killer gets in. However, I know someone who might be able to help us. He used to work for the FBI cyber department, but he's retired now. His name is Henry. Henry Stanton. He's been around forever and knows the old coding much better than I do."

Ethan looked skeptical.

"I've kept in touch with Uncle Henry. He was one of the best, and probably still is. He keeps up with the ever-changing technology. If he can't help us, we'll go directly to my adoptive father, leverage or not."

Ethan appeared to mull that over, then slowly nodded. "Okay. Where does Uncle Henry live? And I thought you didn't have any other relatives?"

Chloe cringed at her mistake. She shouldn't have called him Uncle Henry. That was brushing too close to her sordid past. She thought fast. "He worked with Stan before retiring and I got to know him. He insisted I call him Uncle Henry."

The truth was that Uncle Henry had taken an angry, obnoxious sixteen-year-old under his wing when she started working with the FBI's cyber department. Between Henry, Stan and Betty, she'd slowly turned into a somewhat normal person. She liked to joke that they had loved her right out of her teenage rebellion.

"He lives in the city. I doubt he's home, but I know where to find him."

Ethan blew out a breath and Chloe smiled. Somehow she always exasperated the people she hung around.

"And where would that be?"

Chloe chuckled. "By the time we land and grab a taxi, he'll be at his favorite fishing hole."

Ethan raised a dark eyebrow. "A fishing hole in New York?"

"Yep. A freshwater lake right in Central Park. You can catch black crappie, bass, carp and a few more. It's a catch-and-release program the city offers."

The brow arched higher. "Sounds like you know a thing or two about fishing."

She leaned back in her seat. "Let's just say I have a few hidden talents." In reality, she'd learned a lot about patience and tranquility while fishing with Henry when she was young.

He mumbled something under his breath about hidden talents and hidden weapons, but she closed her eyes. She told Ethan the truth. She'd kept in touch with Henry via computer, but she hadn't visited him in years even though they both lived in New York. The past was catching up with her, and it was time. Past time.

The plane landed. They grabbed a quick bite to eat inside the airport and retrieved their checked weapons. Chloe found a spot for Geordie to do his business and they slipped into a taxi.

She leaned forward from the back seat where they were scrunched together to speak to the cabby. She almost laughed when Geordie licked Ethan on his disgruntled face.

"Drop us off at 72nd Street and Central Park West."

After about twenty minutes, and some creative driving, the cabby came to a shuddering stop and they piled out of the back and grabbed their bags. Ethan paid the driver and he sped off to catch another fare.

She clipped the leash onto Geordie's collar and was taking a step forward when Ethan laid a hand on her arm, effectively stopping her.

"What's wrong?"

He scanned the area. "I'm sure by now the killer knows he has a blank disc. He'll be furious over the fact that we tricked him. We need to find your uncle Henry and get someplace safe. We don't know if he has people on the ground here in New York. It would have been easy to track our air travel."

Chloe's heart pounded at the idea of putting Uncle Henry at risk, and she was still worried about Sarah. Uncle Henry was smart as a whip and a grumpy old codger, and she loved him. "Maybe we should go to his apartment and wait. He doesn't carry a cell phone. He's paranoid about phone programs tracking him."

Ethan shook his head. "We're at risk anywhere. Let's find him, then we'll decide what to do."

Geordie picked up her tension and whimpered. She petted him on the head. "It's okay, boy. Everything will be okay." But that wasn't true. Everything wouldn't be okay until they caught the person who had already killed and didn't seem to have any qualms about killing again.

Chloe took the lead, and five minutes later Ethan whistled when the lake came into view. It was a large lake with pristine waters reflecting the late-afternoon sun. People sat on blankets, and children and dogs ran and played.

"It doesn't feel like we're in the middle of a big city. This lake could very well be in Jackson Hole."

Chloe took a moment to enjoy Ethan's appreciation of the place, then scanned the area for Henry's favorite fishing hole, and there he was, sitting on the bank hunched over a fishing pole. His white hair stood out like a beacon. His hair had been white as long as she'd known him. He always said going prematurely gray was a bad gene in his family. Chloe thought the color was stunning.

Being back at the orphanage had been hard, but this was harder. Chloe and Uncle Henry had always had a unique relationship. Most people didn't get it. She grinned, wondering what Ethan would think.

They worked their way around the lake and she called out because they were coming up behind him. He might be ancient, but he certainly wasn't helpless.

"Hey, you old codger. You caught anything

on the end of that cheap rod you got sticking in the water?"

He didn't turn around. "Better 'n that newfangled rod you fish with." He patted the wooden stool beside him. "Sit down, girl, I've been waitin' on you to show up."

Ethan raised a brow but didn't say anything. Geordie ran past her and she released the leash. The poodle and the old man stared at each other, and Chloe tugged Ethan's arm, pulling them in front of Henry.

The old man looked up. He had a few more wrinkles, but he hadn't changed much. Chloe wanted to give him a big hug though Henry was about as huggable as a ticked-off porcupine.

"I see you still got that prissy dog."

"I see you're still wearing that thirty-year-old fishing shirt that stinks like last week's dirty laundry."

"Can't wash it. You know that. I always catch fish when I wear this shirt and my hat."

In an aside, she spoke to Ethan. "Claims he caught an award-winning sturgeon in Florida one time wearing that shirt and ratty old hat."

Ethan looked at her, curiosity and humor lighting his eyes, and then faced Henry.

"Listen, we're out in the open. We need to go somewhere safe and talk."

It didn't surprise Chloe when Uncle Henry

ignored Ethan and spoke to her. "Heard you got some trouble brewing."

Ethan released an exasperated huff that Chloe ignored.

She studied the older man in front of her, and her heart—the one that was cracking open an inch at a time as she revisited her past—clenched at the new wrinkles she saw lining his face. She should have visited him more often. Hopefully, there would be more fishing days in the future, but Ethan was right. They should get somewhere safe.

She produced a grin. "I see you've been keeping up."

He squinted up at her. "No one will tell me anything these days. I have to keep up for myself."

Which meant Uncle Henry was breaking a few rules by hacking into the FBI computer system.

Time to get serious. "Uncle Henry, we need some help."

Chloe almost laughed when Henry shot Ethan a suspicious look.

"Where'd you pick him up?"

"He's good. Sheriff Ethan Hoyt from Jackson Hole, Wyoming."

Henry snorted as he reeled in his line and

started packing his gear into an old metal fishing box. "You always were one to pick up strays."

Ethan stiffened and she shot him a big grin. His body relaxed and they all headed toward the street. They were about halfway there when Ethan shouted, "Down! Get down!"

SIXTEEN

Across the lake, Ethan saw the sun reflect off something that could be the barrel of a rifle and didn't take any chances. He yelled for everyone to get down. Geordie went crazy barking and Ethan was proved right when Henry dropped his metal fishing box and grabbed his right arm as if he'd taken a bullet.

Chloe didn't hesitate. She pulled her gun out of her jacket pocket, wrapped one arm around Henry and propelled him forward.

"Geordie, close in," she commanded calmly.

The dog quit barking and flanked the other side of Henry. Ethan was so impressed by the efficiency of her movements and her coolness under pressure, he momentarily froze. He could easily fall in love with this secretive, unique woman. He snapped out of that train of thought when she scowled at him.

"Anytime now, Sheriff Hoyt."

Everyone close to them in the park was scat-

tering as fast as they could run. He nodded at
Chloe to move forward and he covered their rear.
When they reached the street, he flagged down a
taxi. When one pulled to the curb, Ethan herded
them forward and Henry looked at him with the
light of battle in his eyes. The man might be ancient, but Ethan thought Henry was almost enjoying himself, even though he'd just been shot.

Ethan scanned the area again before ripping
open the back door of the taxi. Chloe helped
Henry and the dog in, then she squished in beside them and started tending to Henry's arm.

Ethan hopped into the front passenger seat of
the taxi and looked at Chloe for an address. She
rattled it off and the taxi merged into traffic. He
glanced at the back seat. Geordie was in Chloe's
lap—his tongue hanging out.

Chloe was so calm and focused; Ethan didn't
think he'd ever get used to her casual manner
toward danger. He wondered again at what kind
of life she'd lived. "We should take Henry to the
hospital."

Henry ignored him and addressed Chloe. "It's
just a flesh wound. Bullet went straight through.
We should go to my place. You can patch me up.
If you need the kind of help I think you need,
sooner's better than later. I have special equip-
ment at my place."

Ethan glanced at Chloe and saw the worry

in her eyes. Maybe the casual manner she presented was a cover. If it was, she was very good
at it.

Henry must have seen the same flash of
worry, because he released a put-upon huff.
"Fine. There's a retired doc who lives a few
doors down. We'll stop there, let him fix me up."

Ethan was shocked when the taxi pulled up in
front of a high-rise apartment building. It even
had a doorman helping people inside. He shot
Chloe a questioning glance.

Her lips curved upward. "Surprise."

He shook his head. "Stay in the taxi until I
check things out."

He hurried around the hood of the cab, not-
ing they'd both ignored him and piled out of the
vehicle. The doorman rushed forward to open
the door. Henry kept to the side so the doorman
couldn't see his wrapped arm and probably start
asking questions. The man was wily, that was
for sure, and Ethan was beginning to wonder
where the old man got the money to live in an
expensive apartment.

Ethan quickly herded them inside the building. A man dressed in an expensive-looking suit
standing behind a tall desk nodded to Henry as
they passed by. The lobby was more ornate than
Ethan cared for—not his taste—and once again
he wondered about Henry's financial status.

They entered an elevator and Ethan's questions about Henry increased when a man stationed inside the elevator asked which floor. The place was very high-end. Almost as if Henry could hear Ethan's thoughts clicking away, he peered up at him from beneath bushy eyebrows. The old man had a sneaky smile on his face, as if he enjoyed confounding people. "Was married once. Wife's family had money. She left me pretty well off after she passed away. We never had kids. I saved my money and made several good tech investments through the years."

"I didn't ask."

Henry grunted. "Wouldn't be worth your salt as an officer of the law if you weren't wondering."

The rest of the ride was quiet.

They exited the elevator and Chloe helped Henry down the hall. Ethan figured his arm had to be hurting pretty bad by now.

Henry stopped in front of a door and rang the bell. A tall, slim man with salt-and-pepper hair opened the door and glared at Henry. "What have you done this time?"

By now Henry was holding his arm, and quite a bit of blood had seeped through the makeshift wrapping.

"Got myself shot, and I'm in a hurry."

The tall man glared at Ethan, Chloe and the dog, but Henry forwent the introductions.

"You don't wanna know. Just patch me up and I'll be out of your hair in a jiff."

The man Ethan assumed was a doctor raised an imperial brow. "My fee will be your 1986 Barry Bonds baseball card."

Henry took in a sharp breath and released it in short, jerky puffs. "You're a thief."

"And you're a troublemaker. I won't ask why you refuse to go to the hospital."

"Fine," Henry said. "Just patch me up and I'll get the card later."

Ethan couldn't believe Henry was standing in the hall of a high-rent apartment, bleeding, and negotiating a baseball card trade. He looked at Chloe and she shook her head. He got the hint: stay out of it.

Henry slipped a key card into Chloe's hands. "Y'all go on ahead. I'll be there soon." Then he disappeared into the apartment.

They walked two doors down, but before Chloe opened the door, Ethan wondered aloud, "How much is a 1986 Barry Bonds baseball card worth?"

She grinned up at him and her dimples popped. "Over thirty-six hundred dollars."

He almost keeled over at the staggering amount, and his suspicions rose again, but it didn't matter how Henry made his money. They needed a secure place to try to figure out what was on the disc—or rather, Chloe's computer now—and this apartment building was as secure as any for the time being.

Geordie bounded ahead of them after Chloe opened the door, and at a first glance, Ethan decided the apartment itself went with the man more than the location did. A ratty sofa sat beside a very lived in recliner. The huge flat-screen TV mounted on the wall stood in stark contrast with the Hawaiian hula lamp perched on a side table beside the recliner.

The apartment was large and open. It would have been stunning if properly decorated.

Chloe dropped her duffel bag on the floor, took the leash off Geordie and headed down a hallway. When she opened one of the doors and Ethan followed her in, he stopped in his tracks. He'd never seen anything like it.

Chloe kept a tight rein on her emotions as she entered Uncle Henry's private office. She went straight to the main computer, sliding into a chair after her fingers had already started typing.

A strangled sound came from behind her. She glanced over her shoulder. "I told you Uncle Henry worked in the FBI cyber department."

She faced forward again. Time was of the essence. "He likes to keep up."

Chloe felt more than heard Ethan move close behind her. She was becoming more and more tuned in to him, and she didn't know if that was a good thing.

"Is this legal?" he asked. "What Henry is doing? Is it legal? This place looks like a computer center, and are all those screens hanging on the walls showing things going on in different countries?"

Chloe figured Stan tracked everything Henry did and allowed it. "Probably."

"Probably?" he all but shouted in her ear.

She kept typing. "At the moment, what Uncle Henry does in his spare time is none of my concern. This is the most secure system outside of FBI headquarters."

She swiveled the chair around on its rollers. "I should have given the killer the disc with everything on it. I've placed my friends in danger, but it's worse this time. The killer is angry." She closed her mouth and swallowed the fear trying to crawl up her throat. She looked up at Ethan. "H-he shot Henry."

Chloe was a master at concealing her emotions, but this time, it was too much. Ethan looked down at her, then knelt in front of her. She knew he was going to wrap his arms around her before it happened, but she allowed it—no, she wanted it, needed the closeness of another human being. Betty always hugged Chloe when she visited her adoptive parents, but this was different. She needed the comfort Ethan was freely offering.

She heard Geordie whimper in the background as she melted into the strong arms wrapping her in warmth and security. *Security, what an interesting word*, she thought. She had always prided herself on her independence. She could take care of herself, but maybe just this once she'd let someone else carry the load for a few minutes.

He held her close for a short time before pulling back, his strong hands cupping her face. Then slowly, ever so slowly, as if giving her time to object, his lips moved toward hers. She shouldn't let it happen—there was no future for them—but she needed the closeness, just this one time.

His lips touched hers, and they were so soft and gentle. She took what he offered: gentleness in a world of violence, comfort in place of chaos, a promise of what life could be if she were someone else.

Her last thought had her pulling back. His hands fell away and she saw the apology in his eyes. She didn't like it, but life was like that, always snatching the good things away from her.

She made light of the situation, hiding what she longed for deep in her heart. A normal life. "Thanks, I needed that. Let me grab my computer and we'll find out what was on that disc."

Ethan looked as if he wanted to say something; instead, he got to his feet and nodded.

Chloe hopped out of the chair and hurried to her duffel bag where she'd dropped it in the foyer. Pulling the laptop out of the bag, she went back to Uncle Henry's computer room. She shoved the kiss out of her mind. They had to decipher the code and catch the killer before someone else got hurt. Ethan pulled up a chair and Chloe had just plugged her laptop into Henry's secure system when a noise at the front door had Ethan quietly leaving his seat, gun in hand.

She heard Henry's voice and went back to work. She looked up when they came into the room. "You okay?" Henry's arm was in a sling, and he looked a little pale, but other than that, he was his old, feisty self.

"I'm fine," he grumbled. "Can't believe a man of medicine swindled me out of my Barry Bonds card. Thought doctors had a code or something..."

His words trailed off as lines of information filled the big screen in front of Chloe.

"Move over, girl, let me have a crack at this."

He kept talking as Chloe got out of his chair and he slid in. She grabbed another chair and scooted it to his side.

"How did you protect the download?"

Chloe leaned over and watched Henry's arthritic fingers move over the keyboard. "I built a new firewall and closed internet access, hoping the killer wouldn't be able to break through before I could get here."

Henry cackled. "He's been trying, but you did good, girl. He hasn't gotten in so far. Now let's get this information protected and off your laptop, then we can get to work."

Chloe took a deep, grateful breath when the transfer was complete. Henry's system was virtually impenetrable. Not impossible to hack into, but it would give them time to find the killer.

She looked at Ethan, standing a short distance from the desk. His lips were curved in a wry smile.

"This technology is so far beyond me, I feel out of the loop. I'm used to solving crimes the old-fashioned way."

"That's why we have cyber departments in the FBI, to help you guys in the field," Henry responded, his fingers still moving across the keyboard. "Nothing to be ashamed of." But the smugness in Henry's voice said otherwise.

Without taking his eyes off the computer screen, Henry got nosy. "Y'all got something going on I need to know about?"

Chloe frowned, looked around the room, then glared at Henry. "You have cameras in here?"

"Sure do, and me and the doc saw y'all in a lip-lock on my smartphone." He swiveled his chair around and glowered at Ethan. "You hurt my girl and I'll come after you, ya hear? I got more resources than you could ever imagine."

Chloe bit back a grin. Ethan's eyes were darting around the room, no doubt looking for a camera. He'd never find them. Some of the new, experimental cameras were the size of a pinhead.

"That's our business, and I don't appreciate your spying on a private moment." Ethan stared Henry down until Henry turned back to the computer screen. Chloe had to give Ethan credit; he gave Henry as good as he got.

Henry muttered as he worked. "Haven't seen anything like this in a good while."

Chloe scooted her chair closer to the bank of computers. "What is it?"

"Old code. I recognize it from my early days in the FBI. Good thing you came to me. Those young bucks working there now would never have been able to decipher it. It's a lost art."

"Can you break the code?"

Henry snorted. "Piece of cake."

Henry lifted a hand with flourish and hit a final key. Chloe and Ethan moved in closer when the jumbled numbers and symbols changed. They formed lines of ten-digit numbers and Chloe's heart dropped.

"Bank account numbers." She breathed the words and looked at Ethan. At a loss, she asked, "What were my parents involved in?"

Henry snapped his head around. "Your parents? The missionaries?"

Chloe nodded. "Yes."

Ethan jumped in when she finished. "We haven't yet proven they were involved."

Deep in her gut, Chloe knew they were involved. To what extent was the question. She ignored the small voice telling her they didn't love her, that whatever they were involved in was more important to them than she was. She reached out and hugged Henry. "Thank you so much, but we have a lot to do. Are you going to be okay?"

"I just lost my Barry Bonds card. What do you think?"

Chloe hugged him again. "I'll be back around soon." And she'd make sure to visit him more often. There weren't many people she cared about or who cared about her. Henry didn't have many more years left, and she made a promise to herself to go fishing with him as soon as she could.

They were preparing to leave when Henry called after them, "I'll keep digging, and I wanna be invited to the wedding."

SEVENTEEN

Ethan brooded about the kiss while Chloe rounded up Geordie, hooked the leash to his collar and grabbed her duffel bag. She must have picked up on his mood. Before opening the front door, she turned back to him.

"Don't worry about what happened before Henry came in. It didn't mean anything."

She was talking about the kiss, and he was confused about it himself, but he sure didn't like her telling him how he should feel about it.

Stubbornness rooted his feet to the floor. "Speak for yourself." The words were out of his mouth before he realized it. He didn't know what the kiss meant, but he didn't like that it meant nothing to her, and that made the whole thing even more confusing.

He stepped in front of her before she got to the door, but stopped with his hand on the doorknob. "We'll discuss it later."

Her chin lifted. "No, we won't." Her face softened. "Listen, Ethan, you're a squeaky clean type of guy. It would never work, and my life is a mess right now."

It was the sad look in her eyes that did him in. "Tell me your secrets, Chloe, and let me decide whether I can live with them or not."

She stepped away and he felt her withdrawing from him both emotionally and physically. "My past isn't relevant to the case, Sheriff Hoyt. I suggest we get this show on the road. We're getting closer, but the longer it takes to find this maniac, the longer my friends are at risk."

He backed off. He didn't know why he was pushing the issue. It wasn't like he was ready for a relationship anyway, and she definitely wasn't his type. "Fine. I think we should visit your adoptive father. We need help."

She surprised him when she said, "I agree. I'll call Stan, tell him to meet us at his house."

He nodded, went out first and checked the hall. They took the elevator and were in the lobby within minutes. Henry must have been three steps ahead of them and set up the rental car earlier because the guy at the desk pointed out the door.

"There's a rental car waiting."

Ethan shifted his duffel bag on his shoulder and stepped out first. He opened the passenger door of the rental car, and Chloe and Geordie hopped in. He rounded the hood of the vehicle, and the guy who'd delivered the car handed him the keys and headed toward the subway entrance on the corner.

Chloe gave Ethan the address after he slid into the driver's seat. He put it in the GPS and they were on their way. She looked calm, but Ethan had a better feel for her now. Problem was, he didn't know what was going on in that busy mind of hers.

"How far to our destination?"

"Between one and two hours, based on the traffic. Stan and Betty live in Queens. Stan commutes every day."

"Wouldn't it have been quicker to meet him at his office?"

"Not unless you want me to be tied up at the police station for hours. Don't forget I'm a person of interest because a dead body was found in my apartment."

Ethan tapped the steering wheel with his index finger and processed everything that had happened. He thought about Chloe having to revisit her past. A past filled with pain and loss.

"Tell me about Stan and Betty."

Her lips curled in a genuine smile. "Stan looks like a poster child for the FBI. He's tall, muscular but slim, and has salt-and-pepper hair. He's always been firm, but fair. Betty volunteers a lot."

"I'm sure you were a handful."

"Sarcasm, Sheriff?"

"Sorry, I didn't mean to interrupt you. Please go on." He found himself more and more intrigued by Chloe Spencer and wanted to know everything about her.

Chloe stared out the passenger window. "It didn't take but about a year for Stan and Betty to work their magic on me. It was good cop, bad cop. Stan would dole out the punishment when I misbehaved, and Betty would sneak me cookies while I was grounded."

"They sound like good people."

She turned and gave him a fierce look. "They are, and they don't deserve to get hurt because of me or my biological parents. Neither do my friends."

"Chloe, you and your parents aren't the ones at fault here. The killer has sole responsibility for anything that happens."

She turned away again, staring out the window. "We don't know what my parents were involved in." She gave a sardonic laugh. "Maybe I'm just a chip off the old block. It appears as if my parents didn't exactly live in a black-and-white world, either."

Ethan couldn't take it anymore. He reached over and touched her hand, which was lying on her thigh. "Listen to me, you're your own person. You're not your parents or anyone else. God made you unique, and He gave you the option of making your own choices."

She pulled her hand out from under his. "Don't." She took a deep breath. "Just don't."

He experienced a sharp feeling of loss he couldn't explain and didn't even know if he wanted to try. Best to stick to business and forget all the personal stuff.

"Okay, we know the information that was on the disc is bank account numbers and we're getting ready to meet with Stan. Do you think he'll be willing to use FBI resources to help us and not turn you in?"

Her brown eyes flashed. "The letter my mother left me said to contact Stan if I found myself in any kind of unexplainable trouble or danger, and Sarah would know how to reach him. That means my parents knew Stan before they died, which means Stan knows something."

He absorbed that information and placed his hand back over Chloe's. "That doesn't mean anyone betrayed you. It just means you don't have all the information."

"Whatever. We'll find out soon enough."

Ethan hoped there were no more unwanted surprises in store for Chloe. She might appear as tough as shoe leather on the outside, but the

edges of her toughness were beginning to un-
ravel, one piece at a time.

Chloe tensed as Ethan pulled into Stan and
Betty's neighborhood. Because of the killer, she
was being forced to delve into things she'd rather
leave alone, but maybe it was time for everything
to come out in the open so she could live what
most people considered a normal life. In one
form or another, she'd been running since her
parents died. From the fear of being left alone in
the world, and from emotions she'd buried deep
in a place where she'd thought she'd never have
to deal with them.

Those days were over.

They pulled into the driveway of a pretty
Georgian style house, and Chloe opened the
door, got out, stood on the sidewalk and girded
herself for what was to come.

Behind her, she heard Ethan get out of the car.
Then he was trying to coax Geordie from the
back seat. She almost smiled. Almost. She whistled, and Geordie hopped out and came to her
left side. She looked down and petted her dog.

"At least I know I can count on you, my
friend."

Ethan came up on her other side with their
duffel bags in his hands. "For what it's worth,
you can count on me, too."

Chloe felt a moment of remorse. "I'm sorry, Ethan. I shouldn't have involved you in this. I have help now and I can take care of myself. You should go back to Jackson Hole and be with Penny."

He growled, sounding like her dog. "It's a little late for that. I'm involved, so get used to it."

Taken aback, Chloe was caught off guard at the ferocity of his statement. Did he mean get used to him being involved with the case, or with her personally? The red-painted front door flew open, and Chloe decided she didn't have time to worry about that right now.

Dressed in slacks and a top, her hair in an updo, Betty was always prepared for company. Her adoptive mother didn't own a pair of sweats. She considered them slouchy.

Chloe's heart turned over at the love shining out of that slightly rounded face, and when Betty's arms engulfed her in a hug, she fervently hoped she was wrong about her theories.

Betty pulled back and smiled wide. "My dear girl, I'm so glad you're home. Stan called and said you were coming." She stepped back and patted her hair. "And who is this young man?"

Betty probably assumed Ethan was a boyfriend or something. She had to squash that idea before her adoptive mother started planning a wedding. The thought of a wedding depressed her, so Chloe started to speak up. Ethan beat her to the punch.

"We need to take it inside. We're out in the open."

Betty took a step back, and Chloe immediately wanted to erase the look of fear in her adoptive mother's eyes. Betty lived with an FBI agent and she knew what Ethan's statement and tone of voice meant.

Betty glanced nervously around the neighborhood and motioned toward the house. "Come inside where it's safe."

Chloe followed Betty into the house. Warm memories swamped her when she entered the foyer. The entrance table held framed photos of Chloe alone, and others with the three of them. No matter what she discovered today, she had to remember what Stan and Betty had done for her.

As soon as everyone was inside, Betty took charge. "Have you eaten?"

Chloe chuckled when Ethan jumped on the offer. "I could use something to eat."

"Leave your bags here. I have leftover lasagna from last night. It will only take a minute to reheat it."

Chloe wasn't hungry, but she knew it would relax Betty to feed them. Betty loved to cook for and mother anyone or anything that walked through the door. Chloe had always had an affinity for dogs, especially stray ones, and Betty faithfully helped her clean them up, take them to the vet and, of course, feed them.

The memories made her stumble, but she followed Betty and Ethan to the homey restaurant-style kitchen. Betty had every new gadget on the market. Chloe slid into a chair at the solid oak table across from Ethan and grinned when he sniffed the air and breathed deeply.

"Betty cooks from scratch."

He closed his eyes. "I can't remember the last time we ate."

"Airport."

"Yes, I can barely visualize that greasy burger with the sweet aroma of ambrosia now tickling my olfactory senses."

"Why, Sheriff, I had no idea you were so poetic."

His eyes opened and he gazed at her intently. "I can be when the situation warrants it."

Betty beamed, looking at the two of them. The break from Chloe's whirling thoughts was nice, but she didn't want her adoptive mother to get any ideas.

"Yeah, well, I'm sure one day you'll make some woman happy."

Betty frowned when she set two plates in front of them and one on the floor for Geordie. Chloe felt bad for bursting her bubble, but it had to be done. As soon as the killer was caught, Ethan would go back to Jackson Hole, and Chloe would pick up her life where she'd left off. Which reminded her... "I need to check my email. I'll use Stan's computer."

She shoved one last forkful of lasagna into her mouth and stood to head to Stan's office, but time had run out. Stan came through the front door just as she entered the foyer. She looked up and they stared at one another for what felt like an eternity. She couldn't even name the myriad of emotions flooding his face, and she didn't want to.

"We need to talk," he said in that firm voice she remembered all too well from her teenage years, but she wasn't a teenager anymore.

"Yes, we do."

"You told me to trust you, and I have. I've been fielding calls from several agencies who are looking for you."

Chloe's heart was bleeding inside, but she forced herself to say it anyway. "The question is, can I trust you?"

Stan looked as if she'd slapped him, but she held firm. A gasp came from the doorway leading to the kitchen, and Chloe jerked her head toward the sound. Betty's face had gone pale as she stared at Stan.

"Stan? What's going on?"

Ethan stood tall beside Betty, but Chloe ignored him.

"That's what I'm here to find out," Stan said.

Betty's color came flooding back. She moved to Chloe's side, stuck her chest out and defied her husband. "If this involves my daughter, I'm coming, too."

Stan peered at Ethan. "And who is this?"

Ethan moved forward, holding out a hand. "Sheriff Ethan Hoyt."

Stan shook his hand and looked back at Chloe. "Do you want him involved?"

Chloe hesitated only a moment. There was no reason her juvenile past should come up in the conversation. If it did, she'd steer the discussion in another direction. After all they'd been through, she felt she had to include Ethan in the conversation. Taking a deep breath, she said, "Yes, I do. He's been with me since I went to Jackson Hole to hide."

Stan strode down the hall toward his office. Chloe, Betty, Ethan and Geordie followed.

Chloe entered what Stan always referred to as his sanctuary away from the women in the house. It smelled of old leather. She didn't want to have this conversation, but she had no choice. People's lives depended on it.

Ethan pulled the drapes closed. Stan sat behind the desk, Betty and Ethan took the sofa positioned partially in front of the window, and Chloe planted herself in a chair across from Stan.

Stan leaned forward, his elbows on the desktop. "Shall we start with the dead body found in your apartment?"

Her heart heavy, she looked him straight in the eye. "Did you know my biological parents before you adopted me?"

Betty gasped at her question, but Chloe kept her eyes on her adoptive father, searching for the truth. If she still prayed, she would have asked God for it not to be true.

He bowed his head and a knife plunged into her heart.

After what seemed like forever, he looked up and sighed. "Yes, I knew your parents before they died."

The knife went deeper and twisted. "Tell me everything."

Stan looked at Betty, and Chloe heard her sobs, but she kept her gaze on Stan. She would never get through this if she saw Betty crying.

Stan fiddled with a pen lying on his desk. "First, I want you to understand that we adopted you because we fell in love with you, not because of what happened. If we'd met you sooner, we would have taken you when you were younger."

Chloe literally felt Ethan coming to attention

and quickly refocused the conversation. "That's not important. I want to know how you knew my parents."

"Why now? What's happened to make you question everything?"

Chloe gave him credit. Stan was good. Evade the question and fire one of your own. Well, she'd give him something to chew on. "That dead body found in my apartment?" Stan nodded. "It's related to something my parents left me all those years ago, something I just became aware of."

Stan's eyes narrowed. That got his attention. The FBI agent jumped to the fore. "I want the whole story."

She shook her head. "How did you know my parents?"

Stan looked at Ethan and Betty seated on the sofa. "It's classified. We need to have a private conversation."

Chloe gritted her teeth, but slowly relaxed herself. "They stay. How did you know my parents?"

His shoulders slumped. Chloe knew she'd won, but it was a hollow victory.

"Years ago—you would have been a toddler then—one of our agents was handling some company business in Kuwait."

Chloe lifted a brow.

Stan cleared his throat. "The CIA wasn't aware that we were over there. Anyway, our guy was captured and thrown into prison. We needed intel to be able to go in and get him out. We did our research and discovered that your parents were missionaries in the area, and the prison allowed them to take food to the prisoners. Your parents canvassed the area, did a guard count, etc., and slipped several notes to our guy, letting him know we were coming and when."

Chloe tried to take it all in. "How did it end?"

Stan held his hands out. "That's just it. We got our guy out, and your parents moved to another missionary location. The whole operation went like clockwork. The last time I heard from your parents, they were headed home for a furlough to spend time with their daughter. It was a long time after they died that I heard they were killed in the field. I assumed they were murdered by the locals. I also assumed you went to stay with family members.

"When you turned sixteen, Sarah called me out of the blue. Your parents had given her my name as a contact person in case they ran into any kind of trouble while working for us that one time. And you know the rest."

Yes, she did. She had hacked into a bank and transferred money to the orphanage's accounts.

Stan wore a pleading look on his face. "Chloe, I don't know what's going on, but please, let me he—"

Glass shattered as the window in Stan's office exploded. Chloe jumped to her feet and watched in horror as Stan slumped headfirst onto his desk. Her gaze automatically jerked from the bullet's point of entry to the drapes that Ethan had closed. There was a sliver of an opening. Enough for a skilled shooter to aim through.

EIGHTEEN

As soon as he heard the gunshot, Ethan grabbed Betty and pulled her to the floor. He jerked his head sideways to see if Chloe was okay and took a relieved breath when she moved, but wanted to strangle the woman when she started crawling around the corner of the desk.

"Chloe, what do you think you're doing?" he muttered.

She glanced over her shoulder and the tears in her eyes were his undoing.

"It's my fault he was shot. I have to see if he's okay."

Ethan shook his head. "Stay put. I'm calling 911."

"No! Don't you dare make that call. Let me see if he's alive. We'll call his people and they'll take care of this situation."

Fury tore through Ethan. "You're putting Stan's life at risk so you won't be picked up by the police as a person of interest?" Ethan couldn't believe it. He thought he knew Chloe better than that, but evidently not.

She scowled at him, and he had to admit that was better than the tears.

"You're wrong. He needs medical help, but he also needs to be protected from the killer. Let me handle this."

He nodded slowly in understanding. "See if he's breathing, then we'll decide what to do. Be careful. The killer might still have Stan in his sights." He glanced at the slightly open drapes and winced. A careless mistake on his part. He should have been more careful. "I'll get the drapes closed and take care of Betty."

Chloe nodded, and Ethan held his breath as she slowly worked her way behind Stan's chair and snaked an arm up to lay two fingers on his neck.

"His pulse is strong."

The relief in her voice spoke volumes. He reconsidered his previous assessment. Maybe Chloe was right. It would be easy to kill Stan in an ambulance or in the hospital.

"Who do we call?" he asked after he convinced Betty to stay down and quiet, then crawled on the floor and jerked the drapes closed all the way.

Betty sat up and the firmness in her voice surprised Ethan. He would have thought she would be close to hysteria after having seen her husband get shot.

"I know who to call. Give me a phone."

Ethan dug his cell from his pocket and handed it to her.

Betty punched in a number and someone answered.

"Thomas, this is Betty. No, I'm not fine. We have a situation. Stan has been shot and we need to keep it within the agency. We're at home. Yes, please come quickly, and we'll need medical help. Thank you."

Ethan looked at her in a new light. "I see where Chloe gets her backbone."

Betty gave him a fierce look. "I didn't birth her, but she's my daughter and I'll protect her until the day I die."

A warning? Ethan wondered. He would assess Betty's statement later. Right now, they needed to get Stan onto the floor and check out his wounds.

"Chloe?"

"What?"

"The curtains are closed, but we should stay down, just in case. I'm crawling toward you. We're going to get Stan onto the floor. I don't think the shooter would hang around, but we have to be careful."

"Okay."

Her reply was filled with emotion, but she sounded stronger than she had before. Ethan looked at Betty, and she shooed him forward. "I'm fine. Take care of my husband."

Ethan nodded and followed Chloe's path around the desk. He expected to see sadness and self-incrimination written on her face; instead, he found an infuriated woman when he rounded the corner.

"I'm going to find out who did this if it's the last thing I ever do."

The determined comment filled Ethan with dread because he had no doubt that Chloe meant every word she said, even going so far as to risk her life. He wasn't quite sure what was going on between them, but he wanted time to find out.

"We'll talk later. Let's get Stan on the floor."

Chloe nodded and they gently pulled the chair backward, away from the line of fire through the window. Ethan grabbed one of Stan's arms and Chloe took the other. They pulled him forward, then slid him down so his back would be on the floor.

Stan moaned when they moved him. His eyes flicked open as Chloe ran her hands across his chest, following the blood, trying to find the point of entry.

"I'm okay." He coughed. "It's a flesh wound. It burns like fire, but the bullet only skimmed the front of my chest. Got the wind knocked out of me. I must have passed out for a moment."

Stan looked at Chloe and tears fell from her eyes. Ethan wanted to wrap his arms around her in comfort, but he had mixed feelings about her. There were still secrets, and everyone but him seemed to know what they were. She didn't trust him enough to tell him, and any relationship was doomed without trust.

Betty had crawled around the desk, and both women's eyes were filled with tears.

"This is my fault. I shouldn't have brought this to your doorstep," Chloe said while running a hand over Stan's hair.

Stan caught her hand with his and brought it to his lips. He kissed her knuckles. "My darling girl, Betty and I love you. I would have been furious if you hadn't come to us. And Chloe, I'm sorry I didn't tell you or Betty about knowing your parents. We couldn't have children and Betty fell in love with you at first sight. Regardless of that, the information was classified. And in all the time you were with us you never wanted to talk about them anyway, so it worked out for all of us."

Chloe swiped at her tears with her sleeve. "You're right. I didn't want to remember. I've been running my whole life. The killer has made me face what I always wanted to forget, but you know what? I'm glad. It's time I faced my past, though not under these circumstances. Not with people's lives at risk."

Stan tried to sit up, and Chloe gently pushed him back down. "Stay put. Betty called Thomas. Help is on its way."

Stan groaned. "I'll never hear the end of this. Getting shot in my own house."

Chloe's voice sounded gruff and Ethan's heart lurched at the agony in her words. "Yeah, well, that's too bad. Betty and I, we both need you."

Stan closed his eyes as if in prayerful thanks. They flicked open and moisture filled them. "Can you forgive me, Chloe, for withholding the past?"

"Yes, yes I do." Chloe's tone had changed from anguish to a softer, more thankful tone.

Ethan could only imagine how she felt. Having already lost one set of parents, she had come so close to losing Stan, too.

Stan grinned. "Then tell me what's going on before Thomas and the crew gets here. You've kept me in the dark long enough."

Ethan listened intently while Chloe explained everything that had happened from the time she had left New York to the present. He could tell Stan wasn't happy to have been left out of the loop. "It's good that Betty called Thomas instead of the local police. He'll bring someone to patch me up and clear the area. I don't need a hospital." He paused. "We'll contact the police after we have a better handle on the situation." Stan turned his attention toward Ethan. His eyes were full of suspicion. "You've risked your job by not turning Chloe in. Why?"

Ethan didn't know what to say because he wasn't quite sure of the answer himself. He went with the truth, but maybe not all of it. "Chloe threatened to run away if I turned her in. I didn't want her to get killed."

Stan looked at him long and hard, and Ethan squirmed a little under his stare. Stan gave a short nod and Ethan turned away. Shaken after everything that had happened, they got comfortable and waited at least forty-five minutes in silence until the doorbell rang.

Ethan told Betty to stay put, pulled out his gun and opened the door, only to encounter a scowling face.

Uncle Henry, his neighboring doctor friend and a third guy pushed their way in.

"You two can't seem to stay out of trouble. First I get shot, and now this." Henry stopped in front of Ethan and glared. "What kind of a sheriff are you, anyway? This is probably gonna cost me another baseball card."

A tall, distinguished-looking man wearing a dark suit followed the pair in. He held out a hand to Ethan. "Thomas Brady. Stan's my supervisor. I have a man canvassing the area to make sure everything is clear."

Ethan shook his hand and motioned him toward Stan's office. He leaned out the door and scanned the area. It was good Stan's colleagues had brought only one car so as to not alert the neighbors. Just before he closed the door, Geordie darted inside of the house. That was odd. He hadn't even thought about the dog with everything that had happened. Figuring there must be a doggy door somewhere in the house and Geordie had needed a potty break, he closed and locked the door.

Chloe moved out of the way and gave Dr. Kerry room to work. She breathed a sigh of relief when he pronounced it only a flesh wound, just like Stan said. But anger quickly filled her temporary respite when she thought about how close the bullet had come. Stan could have been killed and their last words would have been in anger. It no longer mattered that Stan had known her parents long before he adopted her. She loved Betty and Stan, and nothing would change that.

She wanted this guy caught now more than ever and it had to happen soon. There were too many lives at risk. After the wound was cleaned and dressed, Uncle Henry and Betty helped Stan to the sofa and Chloe assessed the situation. She had the information off the disc, but no idea who the killer was. He knew her biological parents, hence the reference to her mother. A chilling thought occurred. She met Stan's eyes when he looked up. "We need to talk."

Ethan moved to her side. "What is it?" he asked in a low voice.

Ethan never missed anything. She was impressed, but irritation overrode her awe of his keen observation skills.

"We'll talk after everyone leaves."

He nodded in agreement.

Even though he had a sparkle in his eyes, Dr. Kerry gave Betty instructions for wound care and grumbled that everyone needed to start going to the hospital and quit bothering him because he was retired. The sparkle made Chloe think the doctor enjoyed all the attention from high-ranking FBI members. Her impression was solidified when the doctor started bargaining with Uncle Henry for another baseball card.

Henry and the doctor moved their bickering to the foyer, but Thomas Brady hung behind and approached Stan.

"What's this all about, Stan? You know I'll help any way I can."

"Just keep everything under your hat for a few days until I figure a few things out."

Remorse filled Chloe. She was placing Stan in an untenable position. He had a sterling reputation and it would be her fault if that changed.

She stepped forward. "Stan—"

He gave a firm shake of his head and looked back at Thomas, waiting for his answer.

Slowly Thomas said, "I'll keep things under wraps, but please call if you need me."

Stan shook his hand and Thomas left. No one said anything until the door closed behind the trio. Chloe had to try one more time.

"Stan, we should let your team help."

He looked at her with love-filled eyes and Chloe's heart melted.

"Baby girl, you're the most important thing in the world to us. Betty and I believe in you, and we'll help you figure this out." His voice grew stronger. "We're not involving my team until we have some answers. Now, you thought of something. What is it?"

The firm resolve in his chin told Chloe that Stan wouldn't change his mind. She sat beside him on the sofa and wrapped her arms around him. "Thanks," she whispered. Pulling back, she swiped away a tear and took a fortifying breath. Stan wasn't going to like what she had to say.

"Stan, after the incident at the orphanage, the killer made a reference to my birth mother."

He encouraged her to go on. "Yes?"

She braced herself for Stan's reaction. "How many people in the FBI knew my parents helped you in Kuwait?"

Stan fell back against the sofa cushions, a stunned look on his face. "Exactly what are you implying?"

Chloe didn't want it to be true, but nothing else made sense. "Let's say a disgruntled employee at the FBI found out the Bureau used my parents to help you that one time. What if he approached them again under the same guise, to help their country. Maybe this time they were asked to recover a disc by a corrupt agent out for his own gain."

The room stilled. No one said a word for several minutes as the implications of her statement settled in.

Ethan was the first to respond. "It makes sense." He looked at Chloe, and she was moved by the understanding in his eyes. "I don't know what your parents were like, Chloe, but I can only imagine that as missionaries, if called upon to help their country, they wouldn't hesitate."

The statement hung heavy in the air and Chloe's heart started beating fast. A calming hand was laid on her shoulder and she closed her eyes. She would like nothing more than to give in to Ethan's offer of comfort and flee from her tormenting thoughts and the possible reality of her parents' deaths, but that wasn't going to happen, and neither was anything between her and Ethan.

Their lives were so different it would never work. She jerked her head in thanks, then stood. His hand fell away, and she regretted the loss, but this was the way it had to be.

Geordie bumped her hand with his nose and pulled her out of her morose musings. She reached down and petted him, only to see the minuscule camera attached to his collar flashing a red light, which meant it was turned on.

"That's weird."

Ethan leaned over and stared at the tiny device. "What is it?"

"It's a camera, controlled by an app on my smartphone. It shouldn't be turned on."

Before Ethan could inquire about the camera, Chloe hopped off the sofa and pulled her phone out of her jeans pocket. She opened the app and saw that the camera was turned on.

"Huh! The camera must have accidentally been turned on during all the commotion."

Ethan tugged on her arm. "Tell me about this camera."

She became alert at the urgency in his voice. "Why? What is it?"

"Just tell me about the camera."

She threw a hand in the air. "Fine. You know I run a security company." He nodded impatiently.

"Every once in a while, a company pays me extra if they think an employee is doing something they shouldn't, like taking home corporate papers and stuff." He rolled his hand forward in the air, telling her to get on with it. "Anyway, occasionally I sneak Geordie into a situation to check things out before I enter a room or building. I get camera footage, and sometimes that's all we need to prove someone innocent or guilty. Now why all the questions about the camera?"

"Chloe, could he have videoed the killer?"

NINETEEN

Everyone's eyes shifted from the dog to him when Ethan's phone belted out "The Sound of Music," from Penny's favorite movie. He pulled the device from his pocket. "Excuse me. I have to take this. It's my daughter."

Betty's eyebrows rose with the information that he had a daughter as Ethan answered the phone. "Hey, sweetheart." He glanced at his watch. "Are you at Mrs. Denton's? How was school today? Tommy Milton did what?"

Ethan was surprised when the phone was jerked out of his hand. Chloe put the phone to her ear.

"Penny, this is Chloe. Yes, your daddy's fine. He'll be home before you know it. Now, what did Tommy Milton do this time? Really?"

Chloe's lips curved in a smile that he was becoming familiar with—one that said she was up to something.

"And did you do what we discussed? And it

worked? Good girl. I doubt ol' Tommy boy will bother you again. Okay. Here's your father."

Chloe handed the phone to him and he raised a questioning brow. In return, she gave him that mischievous grin of hers and gifted him with a saucy tilt of her head.

"Sorry, pal, that's between us girls."

He spoke into the phone. "Sweetheart, you mind Mrs. Denton and I'll be home as soon as possible. I love you, too."

Ethan disconnected the call and slipped the phone back into his pocket. Betty's close scrutiny of him and Chloe, and the speculation in her eyes, made him feel like a schoolboy.

"How old is your daughter?" Betty asked casually, too casually.

"She's six, going on sixteen."

Everyone chuckled, then Chloe moved things along. "Let me grab my laptop—it has a larger screen than my smartphone. We'll see if Geordie's camera picked up anything useful."

Expectation filled the room as she dug the computer out of her duffel, placed it on Stan's desk and plugged it in. It booted up quickly. Stan stayed on the sofa, but everyone else huddled around the laptop. Chloe clicked on an icon decorated with the picture of an eye—Ethan thought that appropriate—and went into the program. She clicked on devices and there were three videos.

"Each video has a time limit. I could purchase longer time limits, but never had the need."

Ethan held his breath when she opened the first video, then sighed in disappointment when it showed Geordie sniffing the grass.

Chloe clicked on the second video and it showed Geordie running through the front yard, across the street and into the neighbor's front yard. Stan's office also faced that direction, so the neighbor's house would have a view into it.

She opened the third video, and it showed Geordie running around the side of the neighbor's house. Ethan held his breath as the seconds ticked away on the screen. Once again, disappointment filled him until the video showed someone running out the back door of the house. The person wore jeans, but the rest of the clothing was black. The individual turned and looked straight into the camera when Geordie barked, but he had on dark sunglasses and a tan baseball cap. The good news was that they got a partial view of the lower portion of his face.

Ethan grinned at Chloe and she smiled back. He reached down and petted Geordie, who had padded to his side. "Good work, boy."

Chloe hit a bunch of keys on her keyboard and Stan's printer sputtered to life. She grinned at Ethan when he grunted. "Wireless printing."

Stan came to life on the sofa. "Let me see the picture."

Chloe stepped over to the printer and handed it to Stan. "Anyone you recognize beneath the ball cap and sunglasses?"

Stan studied the picture for a moment, then shook his head. "No, but we can have Henry run the picture, see if we can find a match."

Knowing everyone had been hoping for something more, Ethan tried to lighten the mood. "So mighty dog turns cameraman. What else do you two have up your sleeves?"

Chloe sat down beside Stan and leaned back against the sofa, as if she also knew everyone needed a break.

"You'd be surprised."

"Enlighten me."

"Did you know that corporations spy on you every day? Mannequins in retail stores are equipped with facial recognition software. Retailers track your cell phone as you move through the store to assess client behavior.

"The Statue of Liberty has cameras that track people's faces in real time. Vending machines, billboards, you name it—they have cameras. The grocery store? Look behind the display of your favorite product sometime. You might find a hidden camera watching you. All in the name of market research."

Ethan was stunned, but another thought occurred. "Can those cameras be hacked into?"

Chloe gave him a saucy grin and it was good to see her smile. "Sure they can." She quickly sobered. "But it's not legal."

He knew that guilty look. He'd seen it many times on his daughter's face, but he didn't respond. Break was over.

"Stan, do your neighbors work during the day?"

Stan shook his head. "The Stantons are retired. They're down in Florida visiting their grandkids for the week. The house is empty."

"Thomas said he had people clear the area, but I'm going over there to look around outside, see if there's anything to find." It was highly doubtful, but he'd check anyway.

"If someone had given me back my picklocks, we could check inside." Not that she'd really break in. She was done with that part of her life. The picklocks were for emergencies only.

"Chloe," Betty gasped.

With complete innocence stamped on her face, Chloe faced her adoptive mother. "Goes with the job."

Betty took issue. "I thought most of your security business was handled at a distance on your computer."

Ethan rather enjoyed seeing Chloe on the hot seat.

"Well, you never know when there might be an emergency of some sort—say a client's in danger—and I need to get into a house or building."

Betty tsked. "Henry taught you how to use those, didn't he?" Betty scolded Stan. "I told you not to let her work with Henry when she was so young. He was a bad influence."

Ethan pounced on that tantalizing piece of information. "You worked with Henry? When was this?"

Everyone froze and Betty sent Chloe a questioning glance. Chloe barely shook her head, and Betty's lips tightened for a second before she pasted on a big smile.

Ethan's mind was reeling. Had Chloe worked at the FBI?

Chloe cringed at Betty's slip, but she sent her adoptive mother an unspoken message, and Betty, married to a longtime FBI agent, smoothed it over and plowed ahead.

"If you're going to be around for a few days, I insist you stay here. We have four bedrooms upstairs. It won't take long to air the rooms out and get them ready."

Chloe was still jolted from Betty's slip, and it

took a few seconds for her words to penetrate. "No, we can't do that."

Betty propped her hands on both hips. "Yes, you can. When's the last time you had regular meals and a good night's sleep?"

Chloe wanted to choke Ethan when he crossed his arms and gave Betty a puppy-dog look.

"Longer than I want to think about." He grinned at Chloe. "While y'all hash this out, I'm going to the neighbor's house to look around."

No, no, no. Chloe didn't want to face Betty and Stan alone. She knew they had a zillion questions and she wasn't up to facing the firing squad right now. She rose halfway off the sofa. "I'll go with you."

Betty's words stopped her midflight. "No, you won't, Chloe. We saw the intruder fleeing on Geordie's camera. It's not a dangerous situation. I'm sure Ethan can handle it himself."

Chloe sent Ethan a beseeching look, but he grinned and called her dog to accompany him. Maybe she'd send a virus to his computer and make it crash. As soon as the front door closed, Betty started the interrogation.

"Chloe, I don't understand why you didn't come to us when you witnessed the murder."

Chloe turned her head away so she wouldn't see the look of disappointment on Betty's face. "I told you what happened, how I witnessed the murder." She looked up into Betty's loving countenance. "I didn't want to get turned in as a person of interest so I can find out who the killer is before I get all involved in red tape, but there's another reason." Chloe swallowed hard. "The killer threatened Stan."

Her adoptive mother's jaw firmed and she lifted her chin. "I'll not allow anyone to hurt you or Stan."

Tears sprang forth. Chloe stood, wrapped her arms around Betty and whispered in her ear, "You might not be my birth mother, but you're my real mom in every way that counts." It was a pivotal moment in their relationship. It was the first time Chloe had ever called Betty "mom." She pulled back and looked into Betty's forgiving and loving eyes. "I've recently come to realize that I've been running my whole life. Maybe from fear of abandonment, I don't know, but I'm sorry it took me so long to trust that you would never leave or give up on me."

Betty pulled back with a determined twinkle in her eye. "Now that we've cleared that up, what's going on with Ethan?"

Chloe stepped away and played dumb. "You know what's going on. He's helping me find the killer."

Betty tsked again. "Baby girl, I saw the way you looked at each other." She gave Chloe a look that only a mother knew how to give. One that made her want to spill her guts. Well, she might as well go for it. Betty was like a pit bull when she wanted to know something. She never gave up and it would be better to handle it now, while Ethan was outside.

"I like him, if that's what you're asking."

Betty raised a brow.

"Fine. I could probably more than like him, but…"

"But?"

Chloe sighed heavily. "As you guessed earlier, I haven't told him what happened when I was sixteen." Betty started to speak, but Chloe jumped ahead. "It's simple, really. Ethan is a black-and-white sort of guy, and a law enforcement officer to boot, and me, well, I have a sordid past."

Betty shook her head, but Chloe put a stop to the conversation. "Let it go. It would never work between the two of us, even if whatever there is between us got to that point."

Betty turned contemplative. "Have you kissed him?"

Embarrassment caused heat to crawl up her neck, and she didn't answer. Betty got a faraway look in her face. "The first time I kissed Stan, I knew he was the one. We'd been friends for a long time, but I didn't know I loved him until that moment."

Chloe had heard the story many times, but this time it placed an image in her mind of her kissing Ethan and she couldn't shake it off.

Stan came to the rescue. "Betty, I could use another Tylenol if you don't mind."

Betty focused her attention on her injured husband. "Let me run upstairs and grab the bottle."

After she left the room, Stan patted a place on the sofa beside him and Chloe sat down.

"We have plans to make."

Chloe studied him carefully. His pallor was a shade lighter than it should be, but he looked okay. "You sure you're all right?"

"It burns like fire, but it's getting better as we speak." Stan adjusted himself on the sofa.

"Are you sure you don't need to go to the hospital?"

He grimaced. "I'll be fine." His voice filled with grim determination, he locked his jaw and looked at her. "There's a reason I'm not going to the hospital and we're keeping you away from the police."

Chloe's gut started burning. She wasn't sure she wanted to hear what Stan had to say, but she gritted her teeth. "Tell me."

"Chloe, when the FBI asked your parents to help, the director came to me because I work in the cyber department. We're pretty much ignored and considered geeks, unless the field agents need our help. I handled it myself since the director made the request personally. We thought the recruitment went unnoticed."

He took a deep breath. "We know the killer is connected to your parents because he brought up your mother when you were talking to him via your computer at the orphanage, and we know they hid the disc. Only a few people knew they helped the FBI in Kuwait all those years ago." He breathed deeply and took her hand in his. "Chloe, no matter what happens, just know that we love you." Moisture filled his eyes and Chloe swallowed a lump in her throat. "We're family, and nothing will ever change that."

Chloe squeezed his hand. "I love you guys, too." She thought about the bullet that had grazed his chest and anger ripped through her. "And we *will* stop whoever is doing this. I absolutely refuse to lose anyone I love to this greedy person."

TWENTY

Ethan's eyes locked on Chloe when he entered the room. He'd never seen her look so vulnerable. He had only caught the last of their conversation.

"You two okay?"

Chloe cast him a grim look. "We will be when we catch whoever is hurting the people I love." When Ethan grimaced, Chloe asked, "What are you thinking?"

He sent her an apologetic glance. "Our earlier theory about someone recruiting your parents for a second assignment is a good one."

Chloe lifted her chin and Ethan's heart somersaulted. Her body was stiff with tension and her eyes were troubled, like she was waiting for another piece of bad news when her life had already been filled with horrific things.

"Spit it out, Sheriff. I can take it."

He knew she could take it, but a person her

age shouldn't have to deal with so much, most of it when she had been so young.

"What if they weren't asked. What if they were coerced?"

Stan groaned as he tried to straighten up, and Chloe forced him to lean back on the sofa, made sure he was okay.

"It makes sense," Stan agreed with Ethan.

Chloe jumped off the sofa and started pacing the floor. She stopped, took a deep breath and faced Stan.

"What if they were in on it?" Her voice wobbled, and Ethan wanted nothing more than to wrap his arms around her and take away her pain, but he held himself in check.

Stan shook his head. "No, Chloe, they only helped us that one time because a man's life was at stake. Your parents were good people."

Chloe cleared her throat. Ethan realized she was holding herself together by a thread.

"You can't know that for sure." She swallowed. "They left me behind when they went on mission trips. Loving parents would never do that."

"We don't know anything for sure, but we know where to start looking," Stan said.

"Uncle Henry?" Chloe prompted.

Stan grinned. "You know the old sayings 'follow the money,' and 'there's always a paper trail'?"

Ethan nodded.

"Well, there's a better saying in my department. There's always a cyber trail and we're going to follow it. Whoever found out about Chloe's parents helping the company had to have snooped in the FBI files. That's where we'll start. I think the two of you should stay with Henry. He was there when I recruited Chloe's parents, and he knows how to move around in the system without detection." Stan grinned. "He hacks into our system daily, but because he's a trusted former employee, I let him get away with it."

"I have two questions," Ethan said. They both looked at him expectantly.

"One, do you completely trust Henry?" They both nodded. "Okay, is what Henry will be doing legal?"

Chloe and Stan glanced at each other, then Chloe rose from the sofa. She took one of Ethan's hands in hers. "It's legal because Stan will authorize the search. Listen, are you sure you want to stay involved in this? We can handle it from here." A deep feeling of loss engulfed him, then punched him in the gut as he stared into her vulnerable brown eyes. In that instant, he knew he'd do whatever it took to keep Chloe safe. He wasn't willing to go beyond that thought. He just knew he had to do it or he'd regret it the rest of his life.

He pulled his gaze away from hers and looked at Stan. "Tell Betty we'll be at Henry's, and keep yourself safe."

Stan nodded his approval. Betty came rushing into the room with a bottle of Tylenol and a glass of water but stopped in her tracks and smiled when she saw Ethan's and Chloe's hands joined.

Stan intervened. "They're going to Henry's."

Betty looked like she wanted to argue, but Ethan figured she'd lived with an FBI agent long enough to go with the flow.

"Let me pack you up some food. It won't take but a moment." Chloe dropped Ethan's hand and Betty folded her into her arms. Ethan heard Betty whisper, "Please be careful."

As they prepared to walk out the door fifteen minutes later, Ethan's stomach rumbled and Chloe snickered. He handed her the sack filled with food. "Let me go first. You and Geordie stay behind me."

She snorted. "I have more weapons than you do. Maybe I should go first."

He was so glad to hear the sassiness back in her voice that he ignored the taunt. He scanned the area with an experienced eye and motioned for her to hustle to the car.

They loaded up Geordie and were soon out of

Stan's neighborhood and on their way to Henry's high-rise in the city. He smelled something good and glanced at her. She was stuffing some kind of bread into her mouth. His stomach rumbled again, and she took pity on him and handed him a piece.

"My mom makes the best lasagna anywhere around."

Ethan took a bite of the bread and savored the taste of butter and garlic melting in his mouth. After swallowing, he grinned. 'That's the first time I've heard you call her 'mom.'"

Chloe dug through the bag, making it evident she was avoiding his gaze. He looked back at the road.

"Yeah, well, a lot of things are changing." She peered in the rearview mirror and tensed. "There's a truck gaining on us."

Ethan looked up and saw a truck barreling toward them. "Hold on," he yelled before cutting the steering wheel sharply to the right.

Chloe braced herself right before the truck rammed into the back of their car and their vehicle spun out of control. Geordie started barking wildly and Chloe closed her eyes, and then they hit a concrete median. The impact flung her forward, the airbag exploding in her face. The car shuddered, then stilled. Tangled in the nylon fabric, she frantically fought the material until she forced herself to stop and breathe. Sliding the knife from her sleeve, she cut the fabric away, and what she saw horrified her. Ethan's airbag hadn't deployed. He was bleeding from the head and looked unconscious. He groaned, and she released a pent-up breath. He was alive. She heard a whimper from the back of the car that assured her Geordie had also survived the crash.

She was so fixated on Ethan that she didn't realize her door had been torn open until two pairs of hands greedily grabbed her, trying to pull her from the car. Knife in hand, she struck out wildly. One man yelled, but she was dragged out of the vehicle. Before she had a chance to fight back, she slipped the knife back into her sleeve just as someone slapped a cloth over her mouth and nose. *Chloroform*, was her last thought before she passed out.

Chloe awoke slowly. Her brain felt foggy, like it was stuffed with cotton. A sense of self-preservation kept her eyes closed until she gathered her bearings. The recent past came rushing back with tidal-wave force and she swallowed a gasp. Ethan! He had a head injury. How serious was it? And Geordie! In the car, she'd heard him whimper, but was he okay? In that moment, she knew she loved Ethan. Her past no longer mattered. She was willing to take the risk. If he walked away after learning the truth, there was nothing she could do about it, but she was ready to lay her heart on the line.

What if he didn't live long enough for her to tell him how she felt? Panic gripped her chest, but all of a sudden, without warning, a gentle, loving peace stole over her, and she breathed in and out very slowly. It reminded her of a feeling she'd had right after her parents died. Like someone was wrapping their arms around her and telling her everything would be okay. She had rebelled against the feeling all those years ago, but now she embraced it. Without moving her lips, Chloe prayed for the first time since her parents had died.

Lord, I know I haven't been in touch for a very long time, but if You can find it in Your heart to forgive me, I'm asking that Ethan and Geordie will be okay, and that justice will be served today.

She lay there a moment longer, savoring the warmth until a voice pulled her out of the loving bubble she'd been wrapped in. She firmed her resolve. The killer had her, but he wasn't going to win.

"Miss Spencer. You can open your eyes now. I know you're awake."

Before lifting her lids, Chloe tested her hands. They were tied, and so were her feet. She opened her eyes and found herself bound to a desk chair. She took note of her surroundings before peering into Thomas Brady's wild eyes as he braced both hands on the sides of her chair and leaned over her. They were in some sort of an office building. There were some desks scattered around, but no windows. Only a few lights were on, and another man stood in the shadows. She had to stall until she could figure a way out of this situation because no one knew where she was.

"I don't understand," she said in a soothing manner. "Why are you doing this? I thought you were Stan's friend."

A fire lit his eyes, and for a moment she thought he was going to slap her, but he stood and crossed his arms over his chest. The fire turned to calculation.

"You've been a hard woman to find, Miss Spencer, tucked away all those years in that orphanage."

"So you said." Hatred flared in his eyes, but then his lips twisted into a cruel smile. She realized he wanted to tell her what he'd done. Show her how smart he was. His next words proved her right.

"We're a lot alike, you and I." He leaned over her and spittle came out of his mouth when he talked. "We have both lived in the gray area of life." He backed away again and started pacing in front of her.

"You see, it started years ago, when Stan was promoted over me. I had been with the FBI longer than him, and he got my job." He stopped and twisted toward her, and Chloe leaned away from him.

"That job was mine and Stan stole it." He paced once again. "I kept my eye on things, did a little research, and found out about Stan contacting your parents to help them get that fool of an agent out of Kuwait. That's when I realized what a fantastic opportunity I had stumbled upon.

"I waited six months after your parents helped Stan, then approached them, all in the name of helping their country, of course. I had them do a few small things for me, just to make sure they were up to it, then I went for the big score. Their instructions were to steal a disc vital to the safety of our country, and that was actually true. I had solid information from a friend of mine in the CIA about a large amount of money being transferred to a splinter group near where your parents were working. As missionaries, they were able to move in and out of small villages with ease. But then things started to go wrong."

His face turned a mottled red. "I monitored

and rerouted all your parents' phone calls and movements, preventing them from contacting Stan when they finally realized something was wrong. That's when I knew they had become suspicious, when they tried to contact Stan."

"They were innocent," Chloe hissed, and he pivoted toward her. "They didn't know you were corrupt." Chloe closed her eyes. She wanted to weep for all the wasted years blaming her parents and turning her back on God. For all the wasted time she'd considered her parents selfish for leaving her behind while they helped other people. She'd been so wrong about everything.

She opened her eyes and jerked back when putrid breath hit her in the face.

"You want to know how I convinced them to do what I wanted, even after they figured out what was going on?"

Chloe just stared at him.

"I told them if they didn't help me, I'd make sure their beautiful little girl would go to the heaven they so firmly believed in."

Chloe gasped. "No," she whispered. It was too much. Her parents had died trying to save her.

Thomas stood straight again. "Then the innocent missionaries outsmarted me. They gave me a blank disc, same as their daughter did. But I made a grave error in judgment. I got rid of them before I checked the disc."

He got in her face again. "I won't make the same mistake now. I'll have the information on that disc before you die."

She needed to buy more time. "I could have died in the crash and you wouldn't have gotten anything. And why wait so long to come after me?"

He all but snarled. "The men I hired to bring you in almost cost me my money by causing you to crash. They have paid for their mistake. They were only supposed to kidnap you and bring you to me. The reason it took so long for me to come after you is that you're a wily little thing. I looked for years, but couldn't find you. Your parents hid you well, but recently, I stumbled onto an old secure file. It took a long time to figure out the password, but once I got in, I discovered a wealth of information. Stan had buried the file deep, but I beat him."

Thomas sounded pleased with himself.

"Because of the trouble you got into when you were sixteen, there was a complete file on you from the time you were in the orphanage until Stan adopted you and changed your last name."

He sneered. "You were right under my nose the whole time and I didn't even know it."

Chloe's mind worked furiously for a way out of this situation.

"What if I don't give you the information?"

Her heart dropped when he rocked back on his heels and grinned. "I'll kill everyone you know and love. One at a time. And then I'll kill you."

"Like you killed Peter Norris and those two men in Jackson Hole?"

He batted cold-blooded murder away with a flailing hand in the air. "They were a couple of illiterate private investigators I sent to confirm your identity, but when they reported back and started asking suspicious questions, sadly, I had to have them eliminated."

He rolled the chair toward a desk that held a computer and untied her hands. "Now, I want those account numbers, and I know you downloaded the file somewhere because it's no longer on your laptop. I checked. Time to get to work. I have plans to leave the country immediately and live out my life as a wealthy eccentric man in an extravagantly warm place."

She made an effort to buy more time. "It might take a while to break into the system I downloaded it into. And how do you know the numbers are still active and the money is still there?"

He glanced at his watch. "I made sure no one in the splinter terrorist group was left alive, and my friend in the CIA said they never retrieved the money. It's still sitting where it was transferred all those years ago. Now, you have two hours before I take drastic measures."

Chloe closed her eyes and sent up a short prayer. An idea popped into her mind and she placed her fingers on the keyboard. This was going to be tricky with Thomas watching her. After taking a deep breath, she went to work.

TWENTY-ONE

Sirens were blaring when Ethan came to. A paramedic was pushed to the side just as he lifted his head. They had his car door open and Stan leaned inside.

"Are you okay?"

Ethan lifted his arms and tested his legs. Except for a pounding headache and a lot of bruises, he didn't seem to be injured. "Everything seems to be working."

"Let's get you out of the car."

Stan stepped back and two paramedics slowly helped Ethan. After gaining his bearings, he frantically looked back into the vehicle. "Where's Chloe?"

The medical team was checking his body, but he focused his attention on Stan. The man didn't disappoint.

"She was taken."

Ethan didn't even have time to panic before Stan went on. "Henry called me. Someone is trying to hack into his system. We think the killer is forcing Chloe to try to download the information she transferred from her computer into his system."

The police approached, and Stan pulled out his identification. After a short conversation and a promise to stop by the station later, Stan directed the medics to help Ethan to Stan's car.

Ethan grimaced when they eased him inside. Geordie jumped over Ethan's body into the car and he released a sigh of relief that Chloe's faithful friend wasn't injured. Now they had to find Chloe before it was too late.

Stan started the engine as soon as the doors were closed. "You sure you're okay?"

"No, I'm not okay. We have to find Chloe." Ethan heard the fear in his own voice and recognized it as real. He was terrified for Chloe.

Stan pulled onto the highway. "Henry said it looks as if Chloe is trying to place a worm in the computer she's working on so he can trace it back to her location."

"She's smart," Ethan said, and that knowledge gave him hope.

Stan grinned. "Yes, she is. I taught her everything I know, but she surpassed me years ago. Do you love her?"

The question came out of left field, and it punched Ethan in the gut. He did love Chloe, but there was still the matter of the secret she was keeping from him.

"She has secrets," he said slowly, "but I love her no matter what. We can fix whatever she's gotten herself into. That's if we find her in time." He cleared the terror from his throat.

Stan gripped the steering wheel tightly, as if he was making a hard decision. "When Chloe was sixteen and living at the orphanage, she hacked into a bank and transferred a hundred thousand dollars."

"She stole money?" Ethan was surprised that the Chloe he had come to know would do such a thing.

"It's not what you think. The orphanage was in dire need of funds and Chloe took it upon herself to help them."

Ethan barked out a laugh. "Of course she did." That went with the woman he had come to know. A woman who helped little girls like Penny and trained dogs. A woman who encouraged an older lady to sell her cookies online.

Stan sobered. "She went to juvenile hall, but she wasn't there for long after Sarah Rutledge called me."

"You and Betty adopted her."

Stan swallowed hard before he spoke. "Yes, we did, and she's the best thing that ever happened to us."

"We'll get her back, Stan."

They were interrupted by Stan's phone ringing. "I'll get it." Ethan answered and placed the phone on speaker.

"Stan, it's Henry. Something very interesting is happening. It looks like Chloe was trying to leave me a trail so I could trace it back to her, but it's been blocked, and then the strangest thing happened. Someone from a different system snuck in and linked mine with the system Chloe is using. Long story short, I have a location for you."

"Ned?" Ethan breathed.

"What's that?" Henry barked.

"Nothing. Henry, this is Ethan. I'm in the car with Stan." He grabbed a pencil and pad after Stan pointed at the glove compartment. "Give me the address."

Henry sniffed, quoted the address, and said, "You know your way to the FBI building. This guy sure does have gumption, using our office to do his dirty work."

Stan whooped and yelled. "Henry, you're a wonder man. Anything I can ever do for you, just let me know."

"You can buy back my baseball cards, that's what you can do."

"Done!"

Ethan ended the call.

"He's probably in the basement. It's used for storage." Stan shook his head. "A bold move for the killer. It's almost as if he's smugly thumbing his nose at us. Let's go get our girl."

It had been more than an hour, and Thomas hovered over her the entire time, but she got a break when he told the other guy to keep an eye on her and left the room after saying he had to use the can.

She had placed the worm as soon as she'd started, but this was the first chance she'd had to check and see if it had gone through to Henry. She wanted to shout in victory when she slipped into a file and found a message encrypted in a code she and Henry had developed and used years ago.

Hold tight, help is on the way. I've opened the file with the information your captor wants so you can start downloading if you get backed into a corner. Don't worry, I inserted a self-destruct worm if he gets the entire file onto a drive. It will start corroding within minutes, just giving him long enough to see he has the file.

Chloe squashed her excitement and kept typing, acting as if she was frustrated. It was a brilliant move on Henry's part.

Thomas came storming back into the room and jerked her chair away from the desk. "Time's up. I want that file now."

This time he had a gun in his hand, and Chloe knew he wouldn't wait any longer, even though he'd promised her two hours.

She gave him a false grin. "I just got in."

He ran to the computer. "Where? Where is it?"

Chloe carefully nudged him aside and pressed a key. Rows and rows of numbers started scrolling across the screen. Thomas fumbled in his pocket and inserted a thumb drive to back up the download.

He jerked his head toward her. "This time, I'll test the information on another computer before I get rid of you."

Chloe's heart was racing, but she had an ace up her sleeve. Literally. They'd taken her gun while she was unconscious, but her knife was still hidden up her sleeve.

The download complete, Thomas motioned the other man over. A booted laptop was laid on the desktop and Thomas inserted the thumb drive. He smiled when the rows of numbers scrolled across the screen. He removed the thumb drive and pocketed it before turning to face her, gun held in front of him.

"Now it's time to rid myself of what seems

like a lifelong problem. Are you ready to meet your maker?"

Chloe straightened her arm and the knife slipped into her hand.

"I'm ready, but are you?"

She threw the knife in an underhanded move that Henry had taught her and hit Thomas in the arm. He screamed and his gun clattered to the cement floor. He yelled at the other man, "Kill her. Kill her now."

Just as the man raised his arm to shoot, the doors to the room were thrown wide open and a large contingent of men swarmed into the room.

"Drop your weapon. Now!" Somebody yelled.

Chloe fell to the floor, out of the line of fire. It was over quickly. The other man in the room let go of his gun and raised his hands. From her position on the floor, Chloe saw Thomas go for the gun he'd dropped earlier, but Ethan got there first and knocked the weapon away. Stan took over and Ethan rushed to her side. He dropped to the floor and peppered kisses all over her face. When he pulled back, moisture filled his eyes. "Chloe, I love you. Stan told me about your past and I don't care. It's not important." He sobered and stared into her eyes. "I've been so worried about not being able to make another woman happy due to what happened with Sherri, and I know you're a city girl, but we can make it work. I know it in here." He thumped his heart.

Her own heart lodged in her throat, Chloe lifted her chin and gave him a sassy grin. "We've only kissed one time."

Ethan laughed, grabbed her face with both hands and pressed his lips to hers. When he finished, his eyes were shining. "Is that better?"

She grinned. "For starters."

"Does that mean you'll marry me?"

Chloe's heart stopped. "What about Penny? I'm not exactly what you'd call mother material."

Ethan laughed again and got in another quick kiss. "If anyone can handle Penny, it's you."

"Okay."

He looked stunned. "Okay? That's it?"

"Okay, I love you, too. And yes, I'll marry you." She said playfully, "Someone has to teach Penny how to use a computer."

Ethan groaned just as Geordie came flying into the room and jumped into Chloe's arms. Chloe held him close and looked into his eyes. "Geordie, how'd you like to live in Jackson Hole?"

Geordie grunted at Ethan, then wagged his tail. Chloe looked at Ethan with all the love in her heart. "Looks like we'll be moving to Jackson Hole."

EPILOGUE

Six months later...

The day of the wedding dawned bright and sunny. Betty was crying happy tears while fussing over Chloe's gown in a room in the church reserved for the bride. Her mother finally decided everything was perfect and stepped back. Chloe stared at herself in the full-length mirror.

"I can't believe that's me."

Betty blew her nose into a handkerchief. "Of course it's you. You've always been beautiful."

They both looked up when Stan slipped through the door and closed it softly behind him. Chloe thought she saw moisture in his eyes, but it was gone by the time he approached and took both of her hands in his. "I'm so proud of you, sweetheart."

"Thanks, Dad."

It was official. There were definitely tears

in his eyes. Chloe decided to lighten things up. "I appreciate you handling everything with the police."

He grinned. "Well, you *were* working with the FBI to apprehend a criminal." His smile slid away. "Chloe, are you sure this is what you want? Are you happy?"

This time she felt moisture in her own eyes. "Oh, yeah. This is what I want. The only problem is you and Mom will live so far away."

Stan's lips widened. "About that. I've been thinking of retiring anyway, and your mother is anxious to be close to her daughter and new granddaughter."

Chloe's heart beat with happiness. "You're moving to Jackson Hole?" she whispered.

Her parents beamed. "If that's okay with you," Stan said.

Chloe whooped. "You bet it's okay. I can't wait to tell Penny."

And speaking of the little tyrant, Penny came flying through the door, pigtails swinging.

"Grandma, Grandpa, it's almost time. I have the ring right here." She held it up proudly, then gave Chloe a calculating look. "I hope I don't drop it."

Chloe held back a laugh as she looked at the precious little girl. "I hope you don't drop it, either, because I'd hate to spend time looking for the ring. It'd be that much longer before we get cake at the reception."

Penny scrunched up her nose. She knew when she'd been beaten.

The organ started playing the pre-wedding march and Stan stepped to Chloe's side. He offered his elbow. She slipped her arm through his and they locked eyes before following Betty and Penny out of the room.

After descending the stairs at the back of the church, Chloe glanced out the open front doors and caught sight of a huge bearded man wearing scruffy jeans, work boots and a plaid shirt.

Ned!

She thought he was smiling as he threw up a hand in a big wave, but it was hard to tell through the long, bushy beard. She wondered briefly what his story was and why he'd been living on that mountain for the last three years, but her attention was drawn to her future husband as she and her father reached the beginning of the aisle and the wedding march started playing.

Ethan stood tall, looking all handsome in his black tux. He gave her a high-wattage smile, and her heart melted. She'd never believed she could be this happy, but she now knew that God had guided her to this place in time. She gave a brief prayer of thanks and took the first step toward her new life.

* * * * *

If you enjoyed Identity: Classified,
look for Liz Shoaf's first
Love Inspired Suspense title,
Betrayed Birthright.

Find more great reads at
www.LoveInspired.com

Dear Reader,

I love strong, independent women with unique personalities, and rugged, protective men who don't know quite what to think of the women who land on their doorsteps. Throw in a good dose of suspense and danger, an attack-trained poodle, a precocious six-year-old child, and I'm a happy writer. Let me know if you enjoyed reading about Chloe and Ethan's adventures as much as I enjoyed writing them. You can contact me through my website, www.lizshoaf.com.

Liz Shoaf

Get 4 FREE REWARDS!

We'll send you 2 FREE Books plus 2 FREE Mystery Gifts.

Love Inspired® books feature contemporary inspirational romances with Christian characters facing the challenges of life and love.

FREE
Value Over
$20

YES! Please send me 2 FREE Love Inspired® Romance novels and my 2 FREE mystery gifts (gifts are worth about $10 retail). After receiving them, if I don't wish to receive any more books, I can return the shipping statement marked "cancel." If I don't cancel, I will receive 6 brand-new novels every month and be billed just $5.24 for the regular-print edition or $5.74 each for the larger-print edition in the U.S., or $5.74 each for the regular-print edition or $6.24 each for the larger-print edition in Canada. That's a savings of at least 13% off the cover price. It's quite a bargain! Shipping and handling is just 50¢ per book in the U.S. and 75¢ per book in Canada.* I understand that accepting the 2 free books and gifts places me under no obligation to buy anything. I can always return a shipment and cancel at any time. The free books and gifts are mine to keep no matter what I decide.

Choose one: ☐ **Love Inspired® Romance Regular-Print** (105/305 IDN GMY4) ☐ **Love Inspired® Romance Larger-Print** (122/322 IDN GMY4)

Name (please print)

Address _____ Apt. #

City _____ State/Province _____ Zip/Postal Code

Mail to the **Reader Service:**
IN U.S.A.: P.O. Box 1341, Buffalo, NY 14240-8531
IN CANADA: P.O. Box 603, Fort Erie, Ontario L2A 5X3

Want to try 2 free books from another series? Call 1-800-873-8635 or visit www.ReaderService.com.

Get 4 FREE REWARDS!

We'll send you 2 FREE Books plus 2 FREE Mystery Gifts.

Harlequin® Heartwarming™ Larger-Print books feature traditional values of home, family, community and—most of all—love.

FREE Value Over $20

YES! Please send me 2 FREE Harlequin® Heartwarming™ Larger-Print novels and my 2 FREE mystery gifts (gifts worth about $10 retail). After receiving them, if I don't wish to receive any more books, I can return the shipping statement marked "cancel." If I don't cancel, I will receive 4 brand-new larger-print novels every month and be billed just $5.49 per book in the U.S. or $6.24 per book in Canada. That's a savings of at least 19% off the cover price. It's quite a bargain! Shipping and handling is just 50¢ per book in the U.S. and 75¢ per book in Canada.* I understand that accepting the 2 free books and gifts places me under no obligation to buy anything. I can always return a shipment and cancel at any time. The free books and gifts are mine to keep no matter what I decide.

161/361 IDN GMY3

Name (please print)

Address   Apt. #

City   State/Province   Zip/Postal Code

Mail to the Reader Service:
IN U.S.A.: P.O. Box 1341, Buffalo, NY 14240-8531
IN CANADA: P.O. Box 603, Fort Erie, Ontario L2A 5X3

Want to try 2 free books from another series? Call 1-800-873-8635 or visit www.ReaderService.com.

---

*Terms and prices subject to change without notice. Prices do not include sales taxes, which will be charged (if applicable) based on your state or country of residence. Canadian residents will be charged applicable taxes. Offer not valid in Quebec. This offer is limited to one order per household. Books received may not be as shown. Not valid for current subscribers to Harlequin Heartwarming Larger-Print books. All orders subject to approval. Credit or debit balances in a customer's account(s) may be offset by any other outstanding balance owed by or to the customer. Please allow 4 to 6 weeks for delivery. Offer available while quantities last.

Your Privacy—The Reader Service is committed to protecting your privacy. Our Privacy Policy is available online at www.ReaderService.com or upon request from the Reader Service. We make a portion of our mailing list available to reputable third parties that offer products we believe may interest you. If you prefer that we not exchange your name with third parties, or if you wish to clarify or modify your communication preferences, please visit us at www.ReaderService.com/consumerschoice or write to us at Reader Service Preference Service, P.O. Box 9062, Buffalo, NY 14240-9062. Include your complete name and address.

HW19R